There's Nothing I Own That I Want

There's Nothing

by Harrisene Jackson

Own That I Want

PRENTICE-HALL, INC.
Englewood Cliffs, N.J.

To protect the privacy of the individuals involved, the names of many of the people in this autobiography have been changed. • *There's Nothing I Own That I Want*, by Harrisene Jackson • Copyright © 1974 by Harrisene Jackson • All rights reserved. No part of this book may be reproduced in any form or by any means, except for the inclusion of brief quotations in a review, without permission in writing from the publisher. • Printed in the United States of America • Prentice-Hall International, Inc., London • Prentice-Hall of Australia, Pty. Ltd., Sydney • Prentice-Hall of Canada, Ltd., Toronto • Prentice-Hall of India Private Ltd., New Delhi • Prentice-Hall of Japan, Inc., Tokyo

10 9 8 7 6 5 4 3 2 1

Library of Congress Cataloging in Publication Data

Jackson, Harrisene
There's nothing I own that I want.

1. Jackson, Harrisene.   I. Title.
E185.97.J24A37   917.47'1'06960730924 [B]   74-8801
ISBN 0-13-914697-0

INTRODUCTION

On one level, this is the story of a survivor.

On another, it is a story about heroism and loyalty, the kind that is commonplace, though not always visible to us, in the everyday life of black people in this country. Finally, it is about a woman who carries out the commandment: "Love life before the meaning of it."

About five years ago, Harrisene (Penny) Jackson, high-school dropout, practical nurse, mother of three small children, and herself a child of scorn, started out one evening from her apartment in Cunningham Heights to find out from me (I was then Dean of Curricular Guidance at The City College of New York) whether she could become a student again.

On her way through St. Nicholas Park, she was attacked by a hood wielding a knife. She thinks she saved herself from rape by her quick action: With a deft blow to his groin, she knocked her attacker down and fled to the safety of the college library. As soon as she recovered her breath, she resumed her quest. She was accosted a second time by the same assailant, and once more she managed to escape this persistent pursuer. When she reached my office, she discovered that through a misunderstanding we had missed connections. Had Penny Jackson decided there and then to give up her dream, no one could have found fault.

But Penny Jackson had endured much grimmer experiences in her twenty-seven years of beating the odds, and she called to arrange another appointment. This time we met, and as I asked her the routine questions about her educational background, she told her story, simply, calmly, at times even cheerfully. Could she put it down on paper so that I could pass it on to the Admissions Office for evaluation? She said she would. Frankly, I never expected to hear from her again. But her account arrived in the form of a letter, and I knew I would have to share it with others.

I sent it off to THE NATION, where Bob Hatch published it under the title of "A Letter to the Castle" (May 20, 1968). Among the many readers who were deeply touched by the contents of that letter was an editor named Bram Cavin, who invited Penny to write a book for him.

During the next five years, at considerable expense of spirit, Penny Jackson found ways to tell her story. Despite the distractions of a family that now numbers five, despite recurrent physical ailments that sent her to bed, and despite the other demands of daily existence, the letter gradually grew into a manuscript of more than six hundred pages, originally entitled, FILET MIGNON AIN'T FISH, an allusion to an important discovery that Penny made at the age of twenty-eight. That manuscript was condensed by an editor friend, Linda Bearman, into the account you now hold in your hands. Although the organization of the book is hers, the words and the thoughts are Penny Jackson's. Everything is set down just as it was spoken or written by the author between chores and children.

This is a remarkable little book, a testament to the human spirit. In the words of a great writer, such a book can be one of the props, the pillars to help others endure and prevail.

LEO HAMALIAN
Department of English
The City College
City University of New York

There's Nothing I Own That I Want

1 "He's killing Mommy! He's killing Mommy! Hercules is killing Mommy! Somebody help us! Oh, please, won't somebody help us? Mommy! Mommy! Why don't you help us? Oh Mommy, Mommy, please don't die!"

GRAPPLING COUPLE DIE
IN FIVE STORY FALL

Mrs. Catherine Bailey, twenty-seven, and Hercules Roundtree, thirty-three, Negroes, were seen grappling on a fifth-floor fire escape at 1146 Intervale Avenue by a neighbor aroused by a noise at 6:15 A.M.

A moment later, police said, both plunged to their deaths. Mrs. Bailey's four children were asleep at the time. Roundtree lived at 1108 Intervale.

(New York Daily News, July 13, 1947; page 4c)

Lies! Lies! Somebody blew. Some indifferent reporter who was out to get the latest story on how black people only have time to kill each other. I know because I was there and so were my two older sisters and my twin brother. Yes, we were all there, covered with my Mommy's precious blood. From the beginning of her bloody, untimely and undeserving beating until her forced fall and the breaking of her body when it slammed upon that wretched, dirty, unfeeling asphalt sidewalk.

That morning of July 12, 1947, started like any other morning for me. I peed in my bed and made my journey from my tiny "closet-room," which I shared with my two older sisters and my twin brother. I would pitter-patter across our "kitchen-living-room" and past the bathroom (which I no longer needed) and come to the door of my mother's room. I was seeking the warmth of her bed and body. I remember seeing the door down the hall completely torn off the hinges and turning towards my mother's bed. There in the bed was my mother in just a slip and Hercules in an undershirt with his bare ass straddled over Mommy choking the very life out of her. She was crying but struggling with all the life of her body. Then, before I knew what was happening, all of us were in the room trying to help her.

On the night before Hercules murdered Mommy, they had a violent argument and because we feared it was more violent than the other arguments, Letty, our big sister, ran through the kitchen gathering all the sharp utensils and hiding them.

We went and got the knives and scissors and went to defend our mother. But by the time we got back to the room he had dragged her by the throat like a little rag doll out to the window and onto the fire escape. He was beating at her body and with every blow he kept swinging his body around to us and saying, "You next, you next." We tried so hard to help her. We struck with knives and scissors and beat him with our fists and kept screamin', "Mommy, Mommy, fight back. Don't let him kill you! Fight back!" His blood was all over us. Joleen, my middle sister who was eight years old then, plunged a knife into his back and he grabbed at her and said: "You see, Joleen, you didn't kill me! But you're next. I'm going to kill her and all four of you motherfuckers. If I can't have her, then nobody will." Then he got one of the knives we had thrown at him and he put it in my mother's mouth and kept juggin' it down her throat and chokin' her with his massive black hand. I can still see it now and I'll never forget the blood and the sound of the juggin' that knife made against her throat. We were so small and so tiny and so helpless and no fucking match for this giant of a man Hercules.

Then my Aunt Betty came running into the room and tried to push us away. She had a hammer and she kept swinging it at him and she kept saying, "Oh Herc, don't do this. Please don't kill Catherine." But he was too far gone. He kept saying "You next, you next," and I'll never forget those words as long as I live. He grabbed the hammer and struck Aunt Betty in the stomach and from this she later lost an ovary. He took the hammer and began to beat my Mommy in her chest and stomach, each blow crushing her bones. And my Mommy never cried a mumbling word, like Jesus when He was crucified.

She did fight back in her own desperate way. She held on with her arms up over her head to the bars of the fire escape until blood ran from her fingers. She knew she was dying from the brutal beating. But she also knew that by holding on and taking the punishment, the more time there would be for someone to save us, her children whom she loved more than herself.

We battled on. We threw bottles of Griffin shoe

polish at him, butter knives and curses and tiny fists. Mommy got to the fifth-floor fire escape and slipped and was hanging by her bloody, broken fingers. Hercules, bleeding, the knife in his back and his head a bloody pulp, was on his way down the fire escape to finish Mommy and keep true his promise. With a hammer he beat at her battered fingers which were so very long and beautiful before that. He beat her hands loose and she fell to the pavement. Finally she screamed. Her body hit the ground but she was not to die instantly. She was waiting to feel her oldest child, Letty, whom she called "Poogie," pull down her bloodstained slip and hide her nakedness. "Let," she said, "you all right?"

After Hercules had finished with her, he ran up the fire escape lookin' for us. I don't know where we were. He ran up to the roof, not wanting to live, and jumped from the front of the building down to the dirty sidewalk. He died instantly with his brains splattered across the pavement and his naked self exposed to onlookers.

And that's when Catherine Turner Bailey, my most beloved mother, closed her eyes and died in my sister's arms. She knew that her babies were safe and would live.

THE POLICE sirens. The ambulance. The screaming. The crying. The confusion. The shock of it all. I can still feel the gnawing emptiness. All four of us were quickly loaded into a police car. We had to sit on wooden milk boxes because in the 1940's, police cars only had two front seats and a small compartment in the rear.

That trip to the precinct was a crying and sobbing trip. Even the policemen were weeping and trying their best to console us. They tried their damnedest to be kind. We were fed all kinds of goodies . . . Pepsi-Cola, ice cream, and Hostess cupcakes. In between each gulp we wept. Today I cannot eat those particular things without that day flashing across my mind.

When no one came for us, we were taken to the children's shelter at Central Part West on 103rd Street. We were told that our aunt had come to see us. I ran out to see her thinking I would see my Mommy in a wheel chair all bandaged up. I was trying so hard to blot out that experience. It was my Aunt Joan and we wept and sobbed again. I wanted to go home and see Mommy. Aunt Joan couldn't take us that day because she had her two sons and no room and a job herself.

We were left there and issued out like cold cards in a poker game to our respective dormitories, separated from each other and alone with our own personal grief. My bed-wetting was to become worse.

The first morning at that miserable place I got my first real ass-whipping because I didn't know the ropes. Who the hell knows the ropes when they're not yet seven? Someone had stolen my soap and toothbrush and I tried to find out who it was. I didn't realize that, in a jungle like the shelter, when something is stolen from you, you shut your damn mouth and steal from someone else. When the dormitory of girls got through stompin' my ass, I dug what was happening. I stole in order to survive, but only when I was stolen from.

I remember one of the first nights there. I decided to stop wetting the bed and crept out of the dorm. I walked down the hall to the bathroom. In the toilet area were two girls takin' care of business and I swear I wasn't peepin' on them. All I wanted to do was pee to keep from wetting the bed. They both jumped up off the floor and began to molest me. They tried to feel me up and when they found out that I wasn't buying it, they began to beat me and then I fought back. Snatchin', bitin' and, guess what, peeing! Them dykes tried to put my head down the toilet. I kept on fighting and before they finished me off, one the matrons came and broke it up. I never told what happened, but the next day, word got around that the new little girl wasn't takin' no shit.

I was so glad when we went to my Gramma's to prepare for my mother's funeral.

PREPARING for the funeral was sheer pandemonium. The family was arguing, crying, and confused. Gramma and Papa had lived to put the sixth of their nine children into the ground. The funeral was so sad. Mommy looked so peaceful, so alive. She didn't have a trace of her horrible death on her face.

I kept looking in the back of the funeral parlor for my father. That was the first time I can recollect my need for him. I did not know that he was very sick and was mourning my mother's death alone, upstate New York. It was not until very recently that my father found out that we witnessed the murder. Our relatives never told Daddy and we never talked about it because we thought he knew.

If you go back to 1147 Intervale and walk up to the sixth floor, you will find a very poor and sad family of eleven living in our apartment. Dig the rats and the garbage. The door that Hercules tore off has just been jocked up and pieced together. No one has ever repaired that door and it is rotting away, just like my poor mother's body.

THERE was a me before my mother was murdered. There was an I. Harrisene Bailey and Harrison Bailey, Jr. were born six minutes apart on February 10, 1941, at Morrisania Hospital in the Bronx. When my father came to see me at the hospital I was told he said, "Look, her eyes are as big as pennies." So they called me "Penny" and for some reason they nicknamed my brother "Butch." My father's name is, what else, Harrison Senior.

My earliest memories are living in a commune with my grandparents, who were my mother's mother and father. We called her father "Papa," but his name was William Turner, and we called her mother "Gramma," but her name was India Turner. They had migrated, like so many other black families, from the South, looking for the Promised Land. They brought their nine children with them and left their farm in Virginia. They ended up on Eighth Avenue in Harlem. I don't remember the street but I know all of us lived there together as one big happy family with all the aches and pains that any big, happy family would go through.

I used to have fun on my grandmother's sewin' machine. It was one of those old-fashioned sewin' machines that had the pedals down at the bottom. We used to sit in it. We would sneak in there and Gramma would catch us and every day we'd get our butts dusted for playin' in the sewin' machine.

Papa was a vendor and he worked so hard. He never talked much. I only remember that his biggest pastime in the world was sittin' and listenin' to the radio at night, especially the news. He used to push his fruit wagon from sunup to sundown and it's very ironic that I never remember us ever having fruit in the house.

Gramma was a strong-willed woman. She was pure Blackfoot Indian. She was very tall, and had long straight hair which she parted in the middle and plaited in two braids. She went to Abyssinia Baptist Church every Sunday to hear Adam Clayton Powell preach. That's how she got her cookies.

Now I don't know why my grandparents slept in separate rooms. Maybe it was because they had nine kids. But Papa slept in his room and Gramma slept in hers. They didn't communicate verbally much. Kind of silent. But they dug each other because they were together for so many years. But by 1947, they had outlived six of their nine children.

My mother was about five-foot-seven and was very pretty and had a beautiful smile. The only time I never saw that smile was when she was layin' up on four pillows with her latest asthma attack. My mother was very sickly. She was asthmatic. I remember reading a book called *W.A.S.P.* and in one of the chapters Horwitz, the author, states that most kids who lived in the ghetto or in the sinks, or what I jokingly call the asphalt plantation, had asthma and it was psychosomatic. I'm not a doctor so I can't put any truth to that.

My mother was very devoted to us. She used to keep us so neat and clean. She used to hand-sew everything we wore. When we moved from Eighth Avenue to Intervale Avenue up in the Bronx, Daddy didn't move with us. I heard that he was drafted into the army or called back into the army after being out of the reserves for ten years. And that left Mommy with all four of us. He was attached to the 92nd Division and he was one of the many, many night-fighters who liberated Europe during the Second World War. So there was my mother with her asthma and four children, a set of twins among them who were not even a year old.

We must have been on welfare because I remember always seein' that goddamned oatmeal and that rice and that corn meal stamped "Not to be sold . . . Aid to Dependent Children." That always irked me and I don't know why because at six I shouldn't have known the feeling that getting agricultural goods from the government was degrading. Secondly, I didn't like the way the stuff tasted. But, if it's all you've got to eat besides the paint off the windowsills, you eat it and you're happy.

We used to stand up on a chair and cook our own oatmeal while Mommy'd be in the bed, wheezin' her life away, tryin' to smoke asthma cigarettes to stop the gaspin' for breath. She used to sniff this powder she had to burn that was for asthmatic patients. I don't remember her running like I run and play with my kids. I remember that she used to have a thousand little worry wrinkles in her forehead. I worried her to death 'cause I was just a devil. They say when you have twins, one is more aggressive than the other. I was the aggressive one and I used to keep my brother's behind in hot water right along with mine. I used to lead him like the blind leads the blind.

One time my father came to visit us and he brought my mother a two-pound jar of hair pommade and a satin spread. Mommy put this pretty spread on her bed and she left this jar of pommade out where I could reach it. So Daddy took her out to shop and after they left, I said, "Come on Butch, let's go deal with this pommade." So we did. We sat in the middle of Mommy's satin spread and opened up the jar of pommade. When Daddy came in with Mommy he busted our chops so bad. It's an old story around the house and my father still tells it. He beat me first and I was cryin' and rubbin' my legs and then when he beat my brother, Butch, I said, "Don't cry Butch. Daddy's a bad Daddy." We still laugh about it now.

I used to put my brother up to eatin' dog biscuits. Dog biscuits! And one time Mommy was takin' a nap and because I was a devil, we got us some water and we poured it in the middle of the floor and we got undressed and we did the Watusi in the middle of the floor. We got beat again. It never did any good, because the more whippin's we got, the worse I got.

My two older sisters, Letty and Joleen, used to be closer to each other than they were to me and Butch. When my mother had twins, they chose which baby was going to be theirs. I became Joleen's baby and Butch became Letty's. And the only thing I remember is that they were always tryin' to run behind me to keep me from hurting myself because I was always fallin' on my head or doin' something I had no business doin'. We had a 20-foot fence across the street from us and I used to climb it. I'd be all the way up to the top and Mommy'd be lookin' for me, and she'd peek out the fifth-floor window and see her baby on the top of the fence hollerin' and screamin' cause I couldn't get down. But you know, that's how life is. If you're adventurous, then you adventure.

I didn't have any concept of my parents bein' separated. I assumed that Daddy had gone away for a while. I assumed he was in the military which, for a time he was. But eventually he got out and cut hair with my Uncle "Little Boy." They had a barber shop down on 126th Street and 7th Avenue in Harlem. Mommy would give us money and big sister Letty would take us on the trolley to see Daddy. We'd spend the day with him. We used to go to the five and dime and my father had lots of tips in his barber jacket. Joleen used to introduce Daddy to all the women who worked behind the counters. She'd say, "This is my Daddy and he's gonna buy us the whole five-and-dime."

I remember Mrs. Roun'tree, Hercules' mother. She was a little old dark-skinned gray-haired woman. She went to church all the time. She would save graham crackers for us. She sat in her front window which looked out on Intervale Avenue and she'd call us to the window and then run us away from the window. She would say, "What's you little bad children doin' today? Don't you know you're not supposed to be this far down? Your mother goin' to worry about you?" And it sounded like she didn't love us, but that's the black folk way of saying, "I love you."

The last time I saw Mrs. Roun'tree, she was runnin' up the block after Hercules had killed my mother, and their bodies were layin' out on the sidewalk. She came runnin' up screamin' "Oh my God, oh my God. Look what he done. He done killed that girl. He done kill her." It hurt Mrs. Roun'tree so bad that a week later, after Hercules and Mommy had been buried, she was testifyin' in church and she dropped dead. She was such a good woman and she loved her son. Hercules was all right as long as he was sober.

I loved takin' walks with Hercules and Mommy. We'd go to Third Avenue to the great big airy vegetable and fruit market. There were so many people in there and there was this big glass ceiling. We played in the stables where the fruit vendors kept their horses. It reminded us of a haunted house. And we walked down the streets to all the little bitty shops. These are happy memories. But Mommy and Hercules argued that night about Mommy marryin' Hercules and gettin' a divorce from my father. But my mother told Hercules that she felt like she and my father were going to make it. That's what set Hercules off.

2

WE STAYED on and off with Gramma and Papa on Lenox Avenue while the decision was being made as to who would take us and where we were going to live. Most of the time we were at the shelter.

One of the rules at the shelter was that all children were to swim naked up until the age of nine. Being very modest at the tender age of seven, I thought swimmin' in the nude was very humiliating. The male lifeguard, that sick, dirty bastard, used to always be feeling particular girls up. You know, rubbin' them on their behinds and feeling them up in general. I never told 'cause who would believe it? I was determined that he was not going to get next to me and that was the beginning of my asthma attacks.

Everyone had to take a shower before they went into the pool. In the shower, I would put the water on full blast and work up a chill and start to wheeze and presto, I had an attack. I would end up in the infirmary sharing a crib with another child instead of in the swimming pool wriggling away from that bastard lifeguard who was there to protect our lives.

Whenever I got tired of fighting and getting stomped, or whenever I missed my Mommy, I would have an attack and end up in the infirmary.

We were so happy when we spent the weekend

with our grandparents on Lenox Avenue. At least six adults lived in that apartment along with the rats and bedbugs and roaches. I don't give a damn how clean you are. In the slums, rats, roaches, and bedbugs are part of the program. In fact, we used to have staring contests with the rats when my aunt and Gramma were killing them.

We finally went to live with my Aunt Joan. The first thing everyone noticed was that we were full of lice. I swear I don't remember scratching them. I guess we had grown accustomed to them. So every night, for weeks, we'd get the painful kerosene and sharp lice-comb treatment. Finally, hot irons and hair grease killed the lice.

The three years with Aunt Joan's family were fruitful. We learned how to cook, clean, and run a house. They tried to love us and make life bearable. We even went to Atlanta for two summers. But we could never forget that we were Baileys. We were constantly reminded that we were orphans. And we were always hearing that it was Daddy's fault that Mommy was dead.

In 1952 Daddy asked Aunt Joan if he could have us. She let us make the decision. We felt disloyal to everyone in the house, but we had to go with our father. We needed to have someone of our own.

Dad and his new pretty wife, Loretta, lived in a three-room barrack apartment in Shanks Village in Orangeburg, New York. Shanks Village was an army training camp during World War II that had been converted to apartments for veterans. Daddy tried very hard to make a home for us. He worked sixteen hours a day at a pipe factory and then had the nerve to cut hair on weekends. He brought every dime home for Loretta and us.

But hunger really began for us then. My stepmother was really screwed up. She ran with a fast, drinking and loose crowd and squandered my father's money on food and men. When my teacher asked me to add five apples and five apples, I was too busy trying to see how the apples could turn into real ones to eat. The bread man used to feel so sorry for us that he'd leave us all his two-day-old stuff even though the bill wasn't paid. We'd cut holes in our pockets and steal small staples like rice and soap and beans from the village co-op. We'd tie our pants legs at the ankles and roll the cuff to hide the cord. Then the small items would be safe until we got home.

We were left alone many times for days at a time without food or oil for the heater. We used to pile up in bed together, my sisters and brother and Loretta's niece and nephew, and cling together to keep warm. One very cold night, we put some wood in the oil stove and that stove kicked up a storm. The fire department came and cooled the stove off. When they found out how hungry we were, they bought us some food.

We attended Orangeburg Grammar School. We were out a lot because we didn't have many things to wear. Loretta never seemed to think that we needed shoes and panties. But the main reason for staying home was that we were too hungry to go to school.

After a year at Shanks Village, we moved to Nyack, New York. We had a big, spacious white house with furniture, a washer, and all the other things you put into a household. Harmony lasted a few days and then everything got worse. Loretta invited her whole family in on my father. There were always men, liquor, pot, lesbians, winos, and cussin' and hell-raisin' from sunup to sundown. The food problem got worse and there were times when all we had to eat for whole days was a piece of bread.

I had insomnia for four years because our door was never locked and any old riffraff or funky, skunky person would float into our house and I was afraid of being molested. I'd stay awake until daylight and then sleep in school. I was always taking on babysitting and cleaning jobs so I could buy the bare necessities, like food and sanitary napkins. In 1952 we were making our own sanitary napkins out of rags and tissue paper because that broad wouldn't give us money.

In 1955, my father saw his children being destroyed, his money squandered, and his furniture repossessed. Daddy found a room for seventeen dollars a week in Corona and we moved. He was working in a book-binding factory making about fifty dollars a week and this was all he could afford. There were four windows in the room all facing the street on one wall. In a small cornered area was a bed and a little vanity table and shelves for my five-and-ten-cents toilet water. We had a card table to eat on and a big chest for clothes. Daddy an' Butch slept on the couch. Letty was in nursing school and Joleen was with Aunt Joan.

We shared the kitchen and the bathroom with

four other roomers. The two back rooms had new people every few weeks. People fought all night. The place was filled with junkies, prostitutes, drunks, and anybody else who cared to come in. Daddy began to drink heavily then and was gone most of the time. But he worked his ass off and always made sure we had something to eat.

I don't know how I stayed clean from my ghetto surroundings. I stayed in church quite a bit. I taught Sunday School and sang in the choir of a little Baptist church. I went to Newton High School in Elmhurst. I was a bright child, but my emotional problems and environment kept me from reaching up.

But religion served a purpose in my life. Rather than joining the gangs that we had, I used to sing in church. There was a gang in Corona called "The Robins" and even one of my little boyfriends—Jerry Ferguson—belonged to that gang. But I wouldn't join—I just kept goin' to church. It brings me back to a very terrible incident in the year 1955 or 1956. I was on my way to the Mt. Horeb Baptist Church on 108th Street and 34th Avenue, in Corona, where the Reverend Jarvis was the pastor of the church. I used to go to prayer meetings on Tuesday nights and get up and testify and get all my frustrations outa me. I turned on to Jesus years ago. The black people in this country—we get no credit for it, Billy Graham gets it all—we know what it is to turn on to Jesus. That's what I did rather than to run the streets and take dope and just screw. This particular night, I was on my way to church, and a friend of mine, James Alfred, was standing on the sidewalk. He looked up into the sky and saw a red star falling across the sky. He looked at me and took my hand and said, "Penny, you're a good girl. You hold onto your Bible. You're rare, and you ain't hangin' in the streets, like we are."

While I was in the prayer meetin' that night, testifyin' and thankin' God for God, thanking God for life, and thanking Him for protectin' me from the elements that I had to live with, I came out of church and saw all this commotion on 107th and Northern Boulevard. It seems that James Alfred was going with a girl who belonged to a gang called "The Chaplains," and one of the gang members came over to Corona and stabbed James repeatedly in the chest. James ran for a block, up to Northern Boulevard, collapsed, and died while waiting for the ambulance to come. Ambulances don't come too quick in the ghetto. He laid on that sidewalk and he bled to death. That was fifteen or sixteen years ago, and the fifteen-year-old kid who killed him is probably still serving time. James' death was a loss to his parents, who were beautiful people. Mrs. Alfred, less than a year later, was to bring another son into the world who she named James.

So when I turned on to Jesus, it was to stay out of the street, to give some purpose to the life that my mother had given me for a second time. I couldn't say, "Fuck it, I'm gonna throw it away." I couldn't just feed it drugs, prostitute it, I couldn't flush it down the toilet. And even now I can't do nothin' but live my life positively and in hope,

hope that maybe one day the dreams my mother had for me and my brother and sisters, the pain that she suffered, the experience that she passed on to us, will have meaning for my sisters' and brother's children and my children. Every time I want to give up and every time I want to say, "Fuck it, I'm gonna leave this self-made prison I live in," I drop to my knees (not physically but in my mind) and I say, "You are alive, Penny, you are alive; you are a mother, you are not dead. You must not give up. You must not falter. Remember that your mother died twice for you and your brother and sisters, so that you could live and make her hopes and dreams come true in your children." And then the words of a song I learned when I was twelve and belonged to the Pilgrim Baptist Church in Nyack would come to me: "My Mother Died With a Staff in Her Hands."

Well, turning on to Jesus ain't no new thing for colored folks. We been turnin' onto Jesus since the first slave ship—called *Jesus*—brought us here. I don't pray much any more, not like I used to. Maybe it's because I became quite bitter in the last few years, because the older I get the more I see . . . and it ain't pretty. Everything in religion is so commercialized that I just don't want to program my children into that type of religion. I raise my children to be humanistic, to relate to human beings, normally and very sensitively, very giving and very loving, but I ain't raisin' 'em to be no patsies, now.

But I feel that as long as my children haven't seen me mistreat another human being—and they haven't seen me mistreat *any* warm living thing—they're gonna copy me. If you see children mistreating a warm living thing, you can bet your bippy they saw someone very close to them, someone whom they pattern themselves after, mistreat that warm living thing. If it was left up to my kids, I guess they'd bring in every cat that had a hurt paw, any abandoned creature. We got a cat and a dog now, and I can't even feed the kids. And I got nerve enough to have a cat and a dog. But I feel that my children need these warm things around 'em. It's healthy.

But to return to my story. We caught the crabs at an early age. I was fifteen and Joleen, who had left Aunt Joan to live with us, was sixteen. I guess we picked up the crabs from the toilet seat in that place. We went to my aunt's. My aunt, not knowing what else to do, shaved our pubic areas and sprayed us with roach repellent. Years later, we were still suffering from the irritation that the spray caused, but I'll tell you one thing, it got rid of the crabs.

It was at this time of my life that I met my husband, John. Goddamn that Bernice Robbins, one of my school chums. She introduced me to John. He lived with his mother down the block from us on 99th Street and was attending Manhattan College. We used to walk to LaGuardia Airport and watch the airplanes. He told me he was going to be a flier and I would say to myself, "He sure is a crazy nigger. How the hell is he gonna fly an airplane? Black folks don't fly planes."

I don't know what drew me to John. Perhaps it was puppy love, or infatuation, or just that times were so lean for us in the food department and John used to take me, my brother, and Joleen to his house and feed us. Was it out of gratitude or emotional need or physical hunger that I gave up a piece and became pregnant?

That was in May, 1957. When I missed my period, I told John I was pregnant. I was sixteen and he was twenty. If he panicked, I didn't know it. He wanted to get married. I wanted my baby, but I didn't want marriage. I wanted to finish school.

I couldn't have been more than two weeks' pregnant when I developed a pilonidal cyst on the base of my spine. I was operated on immediately at Flushing Hospital. John came to see me every day.

My father, at forty-three, met the eternal love of his life around this time. Wilma Lewis' heart went out to us living in that rat- and roach-infested hole and she told Daddy to bring us to her. She got a room for Daddy and Butch on Boston Road in the Bronx and she prepared a room for me, Joleen, and Joleen's baby, Leslie, in her own place.

We were so fuckin' glad to get out of the hole. M'dear, Wilma's nickname, painted up that tiny room for us and bought us a pull-out couch. It was the first new bed that we had ever slept on. When we got into bed that night after taking baths in a clean bathroom and tub, I jumped into my half of the bed and I jumped up with joy and hollered, "Two sheets! We got two sheets!" We'd only had one sheet to a bed for as long as I could remember. I was so happy that I cried. I threw the thoughts out of my mind about John, my pregnancy, and the pain I was having at the base of my spine from my operation. In spite of myself, I slept a thankful, peaceful sleep.

I decided to continue school at Newtown High School. I knew I would not be back. So I travelled from the Bronx to Elmhurst every day. John continued to visit me and was constantly badgering me to get married. He said he wanted his baby, but he never said he wanted me.

For the summer I went to Wildwood, New Jersey. I was offered a position at a boardinghouse there. I grabbed at the chance because I figured I could work a job and save money for my baby. My father bought me my very first suitcase. It was what I called a "country suitcase," made of cardboard with a stripe pasted on it. I was sixteen, about two months' pregnant, and I still hadn't told my father anything.

I shared a room with Mrs. Henderson, the owner of the boardinghouse. I never told her that I was expecting because I was afraid that she would send me home. I cleaned the bungalows and rooms for my stay there. I also secured a job at the laundry plant down the street. I worked eight hours a day, six days a week, for eighty cents an hour. Because of the heat and the type of work I was doing, my spine wouldn't heal. I would make a trip back to New York once a week to Bayside, Long Island, to get the cyst packed and cleaned out. My doctor kept wondering why it wouldn't heal and I was too tired to tell him.

My pregnancy began to get heavier, but I continued to work and clean and help around for my room and board. Who said women get morning sickness in the mornings? I got mine like clockwork at two thirty in the afternoon at work on the dot.

I received letters from John almost every day. He was in Officers' Training summer camp in Winooski, Vermont. They all said the same thing: He wanted to get married and he wanted his baby. I answered none of his letters. I needed time to think. One morning I received a telegram from John. He had contacted VD.

I was horrified and afraid for my baby. I went to see the doctor in town and he wouldn't touch me. He told me to go home. I was so hurt and embarrassed and afraid. I left Wildwood, my job, and with the money that I had saved, I went back to the Bronx to tell my father about my pregnancy and my case of the claps.

So Daddy took me to the health station up by Clinton Avenue in the Bronx. I guess Daddy was embarrassed, too. There was a big sign outside the door that read "communicable diseases" and cops inside getting their kicks. Those fucking doctors examined me like I was a cow. They thought my vagina was made out of iron. The only person who gave me any kind of kindness was the social worker. But she wanted my father to take John to jail on statutory rape.

Later on that weekend I asked John how he got the dose. He said he picked up a prostitute on Seventh Avenue and took her home on the roof and fucked her. Now he was screwin' me and you'd think that he wouldn't have to pick this broad up and fuck her and pay for it.

WE GOT married that September, 1957. John and I never had sex on a regular basis after that. I used to think my married girl friends were sex fiends because they talked about how they were gettin' some three and four times a week. I thought there was something wrong with them, but then I found out there was something wrong with me.

John and I lived with his mother for the next year and a half. We shared two rooms in a six-room apartment. We slept in the bedroom and she slept in the living room. The ceiling leaked and everybody always had colds and there was no heat and there were icicles on the inside of the toilet. John and I weren't relating at all. Being pregnant at a very early age, or any age, is no reason to get married. But John didn't want his child to be illegitimate and I didn't want to be a burden to my Daddy.

We were really starting out on two left legs. John was trying to finish college but he wanted to drop out. At sixteen, I had sense enough to know that a black male had to have credentials if he wanted to feed his family. So I was helping John by stayin' up nights with him and readin' books that he didn't have time to read and fillin' him in. By this time, he was a Lieutenant Colonel in ROTC. He also had a part-time job at the post office to help pay the rent. I had ran out of the little money I had saved because I had bought John books for school.

Not only was the house cold. My mother-in-law was very cold. There was nothing I could do to make this broad happy. I cooked for her and made tea for her when she came in from the cold. All she would do is get on the phone and tell her friends what a slut I was. She wouldn't even say "hello" to me when she came home. She made me feel like trash, but I never told John because I didn't want him to stop school.

After John finished school I felt like there was no need for me. I remember we used to have one can of stew between us. I would eat a tablespoon to sustain me and give the rest to John. I was the one that was pregnant and really needed the food, but I didn't want John to quit. Whatever we had of a marriage ended when John finished school.

4

THE DAY I went into labor John was doing his midterms so I couldn't tell him. I thought I was ready to do this on my own. At sixteen you're not ready. I thought babies came out of that line on your stomach from your navel down until I took my "Mothers" classes.

My pains were about twenty minutes apart and I had to take the train at nine o'clock in the morning, rush hour. Nobody in the train noticed I was pregnant and having these pains and sweating. Every time the train stopped, the people pushed me closer and closer to the other door on the opposite side. So I was like dead; I could feel the baby back on my spinal cord and when I got to my stop I couldn't get out. I tapped a little old man and I told him that I was havin' a baby and I couldn't get out. He peeked through the crowd and he saw my belly and I pointed to it. He was Italian, 'cause when the train made the next stop, he shouted, "Alla right, everybody, maka soma room, here coma the lady with the baby." So they made a big space and here I came with this big belly. Everybody was laughing but there was snow and ice on the ground and I had to walk back nine blocks to Elmhurst General Hospital.

When I got to the Emergency Room they wouldn't believe that I was in labor. I had to cuss the woman behind the desk before they would pay any attention to me. The men came down from obstetrics and slapped me on a stretcher like I was a piece of nothing. "Here comes another OB," they said. I didn't know what "OB" meant and I thought they were calling me "old bitch." I said, "I ain't no bitch, I'm having a baby," and that's when I found out "OB" stands for "obstetrics."

When I got upstairs they prepped me and about three or four doctors examined me. After they got through diggin' in me and squeezin' my stomach, they decided I should go home. I sat in the waiting room. I knew John wasn't home and I didn't trust Lorna (my mother-in-law). I waited till my pains were ten minutes apart. They took me back to OB and I was in labor for twenty-one more hours. Ten different doctors must have examined me until one broke the membrane to induce labor.

I kept pushin' and pushin' and out popped Coretta. They threw her up on my stomach and said, "It's a girl, Mommy, it's a girl." I thought she was a boy because she was bald so the nurse brought Cor closer and opened up her legs, and said, "It's a girl." And I had bought all blue because I just knew it was going to be a boy. I don't know who the hell I thought I was.

I had so many stitches I didn't know what I was going to do. I was too weak to get out of bed but some nurse put me in a wheelchair and made me take a shower. Five hours later I had the chills. My bladder got infected; my kidneys got infected. I was so sick I couldn't breastfeed Cor in the hospital.

Lorna came to pick me up with one of her

friends. I don't know where John was. I think he went to school that day. He didn't have any tests but he never really took time out to bring me home from nowhere. I took care of the baby. The house was so cold that I used to overdress Cor. She had heat bumps in the middle of February. I caught hell tryin' to breastfeed that child. I could hardly keep my nipple from twindling up like ice but I managed.

One time when Cor was around three months old she was layin' in the middle of the bed with pillows all around her. John was playing with his tape recorder and reading this psychology book. I had to go in the kitchen and asked John to be careful about the tape recorder. Cor was moving around on her belly like she was crawling. But John left her on the bed and the next thing we heard was Cor screaming from a cut she got from falling on top of the tape recorder. I had to spend hours in the City Hospital clinic to get Cor's stitches taken out later. The doctor she had was so old, so crippled, that he could barely get them tweezers right to pull out the stitches.

Another time John was drinking hot coffee and holding the baby at the same time. I told him how unpredictable babies are but he paid no attention to me. The next thing I knew Cor had raised her hand and pulled that whole cup of coffee over her head. I used to say to myself that maybe John didn't know how to be responsible for other people because he was an only child. He only had to take care of himself. His mother worked like a dog every day, but he never went without a pair of shoes.

When Cor was three weeks old I got a job in a dry cleaning store. Turk, who had just come from Greece and owned the business, let me bring my baby with me. I used to feed Cor in the back and he would come by with them nasty old black olives and tell me they were good for the baby. But I just could never take to them black olives. He used to bring me a lot of fish also.

One day I started to run a high fever and the next thing I knew I was in the hospital. I never found out what was wrong with me; you know how evasive doctors are in these city hospitals. Working for Turk, adjusting to being a mother, trying to be a wife (which was the most difficult part), and dealing with Lorna's negativism was just too much. I stayed in the hospital ten days and signed myself out. A few weeks after that I found out I was pregnant with Jennings. I didn't say anything to John because he only had two months before graduation and I didn't want to worry him. John's mother kept saying he wouldn't finish school.

I knew that Lorna wasn't goin' to John's graduation. I tried to tell him gently but he jumped my back, jumped all in my mouth, and told me how negative I was and how his mother wasn't goin' to miss his graduation. John was the first black to receive a commission at Manhattan College. He graduated with all B's under all that stress and strain. The only people who showed up were me and my father who took a day's work off which he couldn't afford and came all the way from the Bronx to

Corona. Lorna got dressed that morning and went to work. Her bitterness and ugliness caused John so much hurt that I don't even think he realized how hurt he was.

After John graduated and I was about four months' pregnant with Jennings, I told John I was going to go crazy if I didn't move. I couldn't have another baby living in the same house with his mother. John deferred his commission for six months and we moved to two rooms in Mrs. Nixon's house, a lady who used to date my father. I used to date her son, Holabird Roderick. Holabird and Harrisene were some names; we could never get together. The rooms were small but they were ours. But John and I grew further and further apart.

He got a job at the Youth Board. I feared more for his life when he was there than when he used to fly planes. We had been married almost two years and I think we had had sex maybe four times. It don't take but two minutes to make a baby. Every once and a while we used to go see his mother only because I was still trying to keep some kind of tie with her. But Mrs. Nixon was more of a grandmother to Cor than Lorna was.

John was beginning to make money then and I remember times when he would go out and buy things that were so ridiculous and then we wouldn't have food in the house. I would tell him the baby needed certain things but he always said that he wanted to spend his money his way. I would even have to ask him for money to buy sanitary napkins after I had Jennings. This was the kind of life we led. He'd do all the shopping and the spending and the buying.

In February John's commission became active and I had to move back to Lorna's in order to save money. I went through the same misery, the same indifference, the same impersonal, unfeeling coldness. Ten days after I got there I went into labor with Jennings. I took Cor to my sister's house, and went to Elmhurst General Hospital, by cab this time. The same intern who delivered Cor delivered Jennings. He came out screaming and kicking and he was the funniest baby I ever saw. He done busted my toochie all up. I had third-degree lacerations and they called in the anesthetist. I woke up six hours later and they were packing me. I don't know how they sewed it back together, but they sewed it.

John sent me a telegram and a big bouquet of flowers from Texas. The flowers were so pretty I thought they were for some VIP. My brother picked me up from the hospital with Jennings and my sister brought Cor back to me the same day that I got home. The same day I was standin' up washing diapers and I kept telling Lorna I was so sick and so faint. I was bleeding bright red blood and pieces of flesh were coming out but I went on taking care of those babies for about six days. My father came by the house to have tea with me. I was coming down the steps with Jennings in my arms, Cor hanging on my right leg, and a big diaper bag somewhere and my father asked me where I thought I was going. I told him how sick I was feeling and he got me in the car and took me to the hospital. The doctor had left the placenta inside of me which meant that all the surgery that had been done was botched. When they went to examine me, I passed out. I was so sick that I thought I was going to die.

5 WELL, I said to myself, if I can go through this hell up here in New York, I can go through the hell with my husband down in Texas. We really missed each other, for what reasons I don't know, but we missed each other. Jennings was twenty days old and Cor was thirteen months and we were on a plane going to Texas. John met us at the airport. It was the first time he was ever on time to get me anywhere.

We were stationed at James Connelly Air Force Base in Waco, which is the heart of Texas. John had rented a bungalow. We kept passin' by all these pretty houses, but we kept on passin' them by. This is when I woke up and found out that I was a nigger. I thought we had made it and we could afford to live any place we wanted to. John was a Second Lieutenant and was makin' a pretty decent salary. But we had to go across the tracks. All the colored people live across the tracks where all the industry is: the flour mill, the this mill, the railroad tracks, the that mill. I asked if there was any base housing. John said the Air Force never constructs enough base housing. So you are on your own. But I was so happy to be with John in that bungalow across the tracks and not with my mother-in-law that I didn't give a damn. I didn't give a damn.

But this is when I had the realization that we

were different. I always thought I was a human being and I always knew that we were Catholic and law-abiding and we struggled so hard to get John through school. I realized that I was a nigger and we were living in a racist country. We were niggers that thought they'd made it because they finished school. I know that a lot of people have told their children that if they go to college they'll be somebody. Well, I raised my babies to think they were somebody before they went to college, because going to college is not going to stop you from being a nigger in a racist society. You see that more and more the minute you're really out in the world and you have your credentials.

This didn't seem to affect John. He always used to say I was negative and I didn't realize what he was talking about until I heard Malcolm X speak in the early sixties. He described the difference between the house nigger and the field nigger. I began to realize that our skin was black, but John was European and I was African. It's easy to have black skin and a European mind, but to have black skin and have an African mind is difficult. You have to fight every day in society because you have taken your blinders off and you look around.

We lived on Hemlock Drive which had the only decent housing open to blacks. The rest of our people lived in hell down there. They tell you if you are an officer's wife you are not supposed to associate with non-commissioned officers and airmen. But my husband was the only officer across them tracks and I was left alone. The only people I had to depend on and be friends with were black people.

The military reflects the racism in these goddamned towns. John had trained on a T33 in Winooski, Vermont, and he wanted to be a pilot. They washed him out of pilot training school. They told him he was too thin and that he had sickle cell anemia. I have three babies from him and if he has sickle cell anemia, nobody's carrying the trait. Now somebody lied. They told him they were afraid that he might pass out at 30,000 miles up in the air. But you see they couldn't afford, and they can't afford now, to have too many black men as pilots because they would automatically become aircraft commanders. The whites that would be under them don't buy that because they go in there with the same racist attitude. I saw a lot of black men almost kill themselves because they didn't make pilot. John went on to Navigator School; he's the type of person who can relate to these people. I think if his son was lynched, he'd find a justifiable reason why some racist did it.

My resentment built up. John used to call it negativism but it wasn't. My husband was a house nigger and I'm a field nigger. I raised hell 'cause I didn't want to live across the tracks. Not because other blacks were living across the tracks, but because I could afford to live where I wanted to live. But we had to live where them bastards told us we had to live. And everytime that claxon went off and we had full alert, Lieutenant John wasn't saying that he wasn't going because he only wanted to protect niggers and Russia was coming over here to drop bombs on white folks.

We had a squadron picnic one day. We went to

Baylor University to look at the bears and went into the park where there were two big signs: "Colored" and "White Only." This was in 1960. So nobody tell me about that bullshit about civil rights. Now the "Colored" side looked like it was where all the sewage came from. The plants were almost dead. On the "White Only" side was grass, pretty trees, clean lake. The only reason we got to see the white side was because we were invited to the squadron picnic.

I left Cor and Jennings home 'cause I didn't want them to go through that bag. I told John that the squadron shouldn't be able to have the picnic and he told me I was being negative again. White folks ain't going to change their minds just 'cause we in the military. When we got there the clouds came over suddenly and it looked like it was going to rain. If there is a devil he must be white. Everybody was there. There must have been eighty people 'cause all the bachelors brought their girlfriends. They hadn't unpacked their lunches because they were trying to be tactful, trying to understand. They knew we couldn't come on their side and here we came. I assume that none of them really noticed the privileges they had because they were born white until this squadron picnic came about. We ended up having the picnic at a Warrant Officer's house.

Bonomi, the Warrant Officer, had a big house. I noticed the difference between the way whites lived and the way we were living. We didn't have any sewers over there across the tracks in Waco, Texas. They dug dugouts in the street and that's where all the sewage went. And when it rained all the shit and piss used to come into those little cottages 'cause they didn't have no foundations. I had to get my broom every time it rained and put it out and disinfect my house. They didn't have any street lights in the black belt and the cops rarely patrolled. I slept with a .45 automatic under my pillow every night my husband was on duty. One night I called the cops because I thought someone was trying to get in my window. This big, big old state trooper, who knew I could shoot, told me in that Texas drawl to make the peepin' tom draw back a nub. That was my protection.

We joined the AAA 'cause we used to travel from Texas to New York when John got thirty days' leave. Now a lot of people think that all black people say "dees," "dems," "doze" and "dats." I'm very schizophrenic. I can and have mastered the King's English since that's what the man wants me to do. I called up and very nasally told the people at AAA that I wanted to find out details on how you could join, how much the dues were, and how we could go about getting all the material that we would need to introduce us to the AAA. They told me I'd have to come down and pick up the magazines and the catalogs that would tell us where we could stay.

When I walked into that office and that woman realized that I was black, she reached under the desk and on top of the AAA book that was about two and a half inches thick, she placed a little book that was about half an inch thick and gave them both to me. The little book showed us where we could stay. Now we paid the same dues to AAA to map our route. My husband was in the United States Air Force; he was a gentleman and an officer. And there's two places in St. Louis and Springfield, Missouri, that can rest our heads and both of them are whorehouses. The truth. We used to pass tens and tens of motels, but since they weren't in the colored book we couldn't stay there. The places where we could stay were houses for transients and we would always be taken way to the back where all the illicit selling of flesh and drugs was going on. That's where I had to take my babies.

John even drove one time from Waco, Texas, to Chicago, Illinois, without stopping and had a heart attack. He had pericarditis of the heart at twenty-two years old because we couldn't find a decent place to stay. Now damn if I was negative. I wasn't negative, I was mad as ten bitches and I kept telling John I'd raise hell about these things and he kept telling me I was negative. I mean we used to travel cross-country with babies and I had to worry about things like car potties, cleanser, bleach. I had to cook enough food that wasn't perishable so that we would have enough to eat and we would all get constipated 'cause the places where niggers can shit is any gas station where you'll spend your money to get gas with rest rooms that have so much shit and flies that you hold your bowel movements. This is what we went through when we went cross-country to visit our families. I once begged a lady managing a hotel in Dayton, Ohio, to let us rent a room and that we would leave early in the morning. She told me, very saccharine-sweet-like, that she was sorry but had forgotten to turn the "vacancy" light off. That motel wasn't on the colored people's AAA book. It's still the same old plantation.

We stayed in Waco, Texas, until 1961. I was twenty, with two children. John was sent to San Antonio, Texas, to Lackland Air Force Base. We were only there for about ninety days and that's when I became even more bitter. We lucked up on base housing; they call it wherry housing. I was the only black officer's wife on the whole base. I was so lonesome and I sought out my own people and my own culture and my own customs. Whenever I had to get my hair pressed, I had to find somebody that pressed hair. I don't have that problem now, because I wear my hair natural. I don't want them bastards to love me no more. I don't want to look like them no more. I like me the way I look and if they don't like my bushy hairdo, they can go take a trip.

I used to make friends with the little children because I seemed to communicate with them better. They were more sincere. The kids used to come to my house every afternoon after the siesta we all had to take because the sun is so hot in Texas. I used to make punch and put fruit and all kinds of goodies in it, fruit cocktail and fresh oranges, and the kids named it "Penny Punch." I made 'em brownies and chocolate chip cookies and they would come by and play with Cor and Jennings.

There was a little girl about eight years old named Mollie. She had the cutest little freckled face and turned-up nose and long, blonde hair. She came to my house every day and played with Jennings and Cor in the little play yard. She would put them on the see-saw and the sliding board. One day she asked me if she could give the kids a bath. I put the children in the tub and I went in the bedroom to fold diapers and about fifteen minutes later she came back to the bedroom. She was so flushed. She said she had been washing the kids for fifteen minutes and still couldn't get the dirt off. I was so surprised that I laughed. Here she was almost nine years old and didn't know that there were black people. I taught my children to relate to colors of skin like flavors of ice cream. We were chocolate and Mollie was vanilla and there were strawberry people and butterscotch people. This made it easier for my children to differentiate the colors of people. They just knew they were different flavors of ice cream but they were all people. I had to explain to Mollie that Cor and Jennings were chocolate and that I was chocolate and their father was chocolate.

On this particular day Mollie had stayed too late and it was dark. I took her home. Her house smelled like a beer garden. Her father, a captain, was sitting in the corner of the living room and her mother was upstairs. They knew that she used to come to my house 'cause she used to talk about playing with the kids all the time. When Mollie introduced me to her parents and they found out I was chocolate, the look on their faces, a look that most of us black people are very used to, told me that poor little kid would never be back to my house.

The next day after we took our naps, I let the

kids out to play. I noticed that there weren't any kids in the playground. I made cookies and punch and nobody came. After the children had been out about forty-five minutes, I saw Mollie over in the park playing. Cor, who wasn't quite two yet, saw Mollie and ran over to her and pulled her dress and wanted to play with her. This little kid turned around with the most venomous, vicious look on her face and knocked Cor down and told her to go away 'cause she couldn't play with her anymore. Mollie said her mommy told her Cor was a nigger. I was so hurt that I wanted to take that kid and beat her ass, but I repressed my feelings. I ran and got my babies and Cor was crying and Jennings was crying. I got back to the house, put the kids in bed, and was on my way to smack some evilness out of Mollie's mother when I met one of the white officer's wives who lived next door. She had overheard the whole episode and knew what I wanted to do. She told me not to lower myself because there are rotten apples in every bushel. It's people like this lady who have kept me from going over the line and becoming a black racist.

But I just wanted to strike out at all white people. I had gotten so racist that I didn't want to go to the store and deal with the storekeeper. Now the storekeeper never did anything to me, but all I saw was his white skin, that's all. I'd walk down the streets and I'd want to smack anybody that was white. This was destroying my personality. I was becoming ugly and I knew that if I continued to be like this my children would never grow up straight and tall. They'd grow up all bent and ugly. So I had to get out of this. I was putting up a shield against my will. Society forced me to be like this.

I couldn't totally and completely be an officer's wife. I had to associate with blacks because they were my people. I knew white people didn't want me in their houses because I used to pass them and I'd hear them buzz. I know they were talking about the black officer's wife, the nigger that must have slipped through. John had one up on those bastards 'cause a lot of them didn't have college degrees and they still didn't think he was good enough. Also, I didn't know how to buy clothes and I wasn't interested in sitting around and playing bridge and going to hat-and-glove affairs and sitting there and bullshitting because it was a waste of time to me. I had more fun with my two little kids. I didn't want to put them in the nursery so they could call somebody else "Mamma" and I could sit in the officers' wives' club and wrap my legs around a bar stool and get drunk. I didn't fit it, so while we were at Lackland I just didn't have many friends.

The only people I really knew were the few blacks I met and that's where I used to go to get my hair pressed 'cause they didn't have a beauty parlor in town. I learned how to cut hair, cut my husband's hair, because the white barbers on the base couldn't cut black hair and this was in the early sixties. I used to go across the aisle that separated the officers' quarters from the NCO quarters so often that one day a flyer was passed around. It subtly suggested that officers and NCO's should not socialize with one another. The day after I read that, I dressed my kids in red and I got dressed in red so that them people couldn't miss me walking across those streets that segregated the officers from the NCO's. I continued to associate with NCO's until we left.

We had not been at Lackland for more than a month when I heard a little knock at the door. It was Roger Wilcox, a first Lieutenant from Saginaw, Michigan. I thought either he was lookin' to get into my pants or he wanted to tell people that some of his best friends were "colored." He turned out to be one of the nicest guys in the world. He used to come to our house every night for dinner and he used to love my corn bread. He would eat it like it was candy.

About two weeks before we were ready to leave Lackland Air Force Base we had a party. Roger came and the people next door came and the rest of the people that were there were black. Some of the airmen there, some brothers, were telling us about Salina, Kansas, which was the next town we were going to. They said the town was racist and when we pulled into town we should look for tracks 'cause that's where all the niggers live. We were laughing about this to keep from crying but we noticed that Roger had heard us and we dropped the conversation. Roger decided that he wanted to travel with us to Salina. I tried to deter him but he insisted. He figured since we all had to go to Salina, we might as well travel together. "What's the difference?" he said. "We all belong to AAA and have our routes mapped out."

Roger watched me get our things ready to leave. We had to clean the apartment so it would pass the white-glove test. The apartment had to be so clean that when the housing people came to check it out by running white gloves across the tops of the stove and doors, nothing would show up on the gloves. Roger saw me packing cleanser and cooking chicken and eggs. He couldn't understand why I was doing this since he thought we could stop at a restaurant when we were hungry and check into a motel when we were sleepy. He didn't know what black people go through when they travel the highways of the United States of America. I had to show him the two AAA books. I think he took it harder than we did since we were used to living nigger. He didn't know what it was all about. Instead of eating a full meal in them fucked-up restaurants or sleeping in a decent bed, he stayed on the road with us. He was used to eating regular meals and when he managed to eat a boiled egg or a snack like we did, he ended up throwing up. He was as sick as a dog because he never pushed a trip like this without being able to sit and eat and relax.

We pulled in Salina, Kansas, around four o'clock in the morning. I couldn't believe it, but Roger and John were able to get us rooms at the Lamar Hotel. Our rooms were on the fourth floor all the way in the back where the prostitutes worked or where people just came in overnight. Roger watched me clean the sinks and toilets and wipe off the headboards on the beds where the babies might put their mouths. It's a good thing I did all these things 'cause after working as a maid in a motel I learned a maid can't clean the toilets like they should be cleaned 'cause its pretty damn hard to clean fifteen rooms in seven hours. Anyway, this is what I had to do after being on the fucking road for two days without stopping except to pee. We tested out the beds and they all had big sinks. John had to sleep in a bed with one of the babies and I had to sleep in a bed with the other baby 'cause two grown people on those rotten mattresses would never do.

Roger and John went out every day for a place for us to live. Roger stayed at the hotel with us for about two days until he got a room in bachelor officers' quarters. There was no housing on base for us. I don't know if the military does this on purpose or what. But if they got enough money to throw away on them bullshit X-100's that broke up, that cost four million dollars apiece to build, then why the fuck can't they have enough housing? I'm not just saying they should have housing for blacks who are going to have problems in segregated towns either.

We couldn't afford to buy the food in the dining room of the hotel because it was too expensive. Some of the elevator men used to slip milk up to us. I became friendly with the day clerk at the front desk whose husband was also in the military. We got along fabulously and it wasn't because we were both military wives but because she knew what we were going through. I would tell her how hostile I was getting toward white people and how I didn't want to be this way, frowning at people that never did shit to me. I asked her why they were doing this to us. Why didn't they give us a break? We didn't want to marry their sons and daughters. Ike, that's what everybody called her, told me I wasn't imagining things. She said they do put blacks in designated areas in the hotels so that the white people who came in wouldn't have to deal with too many blacks except for the ones that work in the kitchen and did the cleaning and all this sort of bullshit.

Roger used to come in so frustrated. He was more aware than John was of the shit that was going on. John always has been one of these people who'd rather stick his head in the sand like an ostrich than really accept the fact that this country, goddamn it, is racist and there are just a handful of people that are human. I mean the racist stares are enough to kill you. If stares could kill, every nigger in this country would be dead. You get it every day and you know it. The only thing that really saved me while we were in that hotel was Ike. Roger would make calls about houses for us and find out if the people rentin' objected to blacks. They would tell him they were sorry but it was the neighbors next door who objected, but you can be sure these people didn't want no niggers in their house either.

Finally we found a place in a nearby village. When we moved in there were roaches so big that they were flying off the walls. There were lice in the rugs. Now white people had moved out of this house but this is what we were up against. That night poor little Roger and me and John stayed up all night fumigating that place. We had to do it with our kids in the house because we couldn't afford another day at that hotel. About four o'clock that morning, when we got through trying to get rid of the roaches and the fleas and everything else, there I was again left alone and John was off on temporary duty, TDY they call it, for thirty days to Alaska. He was still going through training.

We got to Kansas when I wasn't quite twenty and we stayed there for two years. John and I separated more and more psychologically. We slept in the same bed, but what the fuck, we didn't screw. I used to masturbate, laying right next to my husband, to keep from going out in the street and sleeping with somebody else. There were a whole lot of handsome, young airmen on that base. I could've had me a ball and still stayed Lieutenant John's wife 'cause he didn't give a damn what I did. But I thought I was supposed to keep myself unto him so long as we both shall live.

And again, John wouldn't buy food. He'd come home with two albums that cost twenty-five dollars and there was nothing but a quart of milk in the refrigerator. Or he'd come in with two South African lobster tails when there was no milk in the refrigerator. I couldn't understand this; I couldn't accept this. Then there was my second operation. You could see a cleft in my stomach and I knew I had a hernia. Every time I went to the bathroom I'd feel like my insides were coming out. Every time I sneezed, if I didn't hold myself, it was just like ripping my stomach out. I had to have surgery. The day I was prepared to go into surgery John told me that he was going into the bullpen (the Air Force Alert Shack) two days after my surgery. I hit the roof and acted like the typical Sapphire. John always had a knack of disappearing when I needed him most.

I remember being taken to surgery and seeing this doctor for the first time. They put Sodium Pentothal in my arm and told me to count from ninety-nine backwards. The last thing that was on my mind was that the doctor was goin' to cut "KKK" on my stomach because he was from Mississippi. When I was coming out of the recovery room I peeked underneath my bandage and saw I had an incision from between my breasts all the way down to my navel. I started hollering and it felt like my guts were ripping out. Every time I've had an examination since then, any doctor I've had asks me where I got that scar from. I'd like to tell them it was my initiation into my tribe in Africa, but I tell them that the doctor who did the surgery told me there was a muscle separation. And a lot of them ask me what the hell is that. I don't know what that doctor did. Maybe he did an exploratory to see what makes me function and take so much physically when perhaps his wife couldn't. I hope that when he was in there he didn't take something that I'll ever need.

To get rid of post-surgery depression and pretend that I didn't mind that my husband wasn't visiting me, I used to race down the hall in a wheelchair, with this little major who had just had a gall bladder operation. I used to sit in the room with another patient who had a tracheotomy done and watch television. One day we watched the Harlem Globetrotters and you should have seen me trying to hold my stitches in my stomach and him holding his neck while we laughed. I used to take care of a little black girl in pediatrics 'cause nobody knew how to wash her hair, brush it, and braid it.

But I didn't have any cigarettes, I didn't have anything. I was really miserable. I felt embarrassed because I was an officer's wife and I didn't have any money to buy cigarettes. One day I was having a crying spell. I was a twenty-year-old kid worrying about her children, and was all taped up with stitches galore on my body. I was also developing pneumonia. Lieutenant Cohen, a nurse and a friend of mine, called John at home and told him that if he didn't get here fast to see me, she was going to come and get him. Twenty minutes later John came in with the wrong brand of cigarettes. He didn't even remember what I smoked and that hurt my feelings. I told him off and when he left Lieutenant Cohen went downstairs and bought me some hamburgers and a malt and we sat up in the solarium and had a ball till about twelve o'clock at night.

The doctor wanted me to stay in the hospital for another week but I told him I couldn't. I had to go home and take care of my babies. John picked me up and I couldn't even lift my foot half an inch in front of me. When we got home I asked him to please fix me some hot soup. I thought it would make me feel better. But he had just made First Lieutenant and was sewing his bars on and he was oblivious to everything but the Air Force. He didn't give a damn. When I was getting undressed and John saw the surgery for the first time, he told me how ugly it was. Few stomachs look as bad as mine. Honey, I could tell you how to get to China with the lines on my belly. But John's remarks made me frigid and I would never undress in front of him until we put the lights out.

At three o'clock that morning John was on his way to Alaska on TDY. He left me with a two-year-old, a three-year-old, a house that looked like hell because no one had washed a dish in nine days. That morning I was out in the snow ten days after major surgery taking clothes off the line which I hung the day before I left for the hospital. There was no food in the house so I got in the car to go to the market. We had a Peugeot at the time with a stick shift and a clutch. I didn't realize how I needed my stomach muscles until I turned on the ignition and tried to shift that gear into first. The pain just ripped through me till I thought I was going to faint. And I sat in that car and cried like a baby, not only because I was hurtin', but because I wasn't independent enough to drive that damn car out to the commissary. I must have thought I was superwoman because I thought I was going shopping.

I dragged myself back into the house and called up Roger. I asked him to pick up food. I told him what to get and he went to get it. We didn't discuss John. The only time he ever injected himself into our business was when I needed fifteen dollars to file for my divorce. He gave it to me. This was a big decision for me to make. John and I had been through so much and I was scared because I knew what was out on these streets. But I saw a lawyer and sued John for extreme cruelty and neglect. But John didn't want to go. I had to get the sheriff and a court order to have him moved. John asked me to give him another chance. What else could I do? Physically I was in bad shape and I had two children. I was also fifteen hundred miles from home. So we tried again.

6

ABOUT two months later John went on TDY again. He called me up on the SAC Line which is the military line that the guys away on TDY can use for about two minutes. John called me up, I'll never forget, October 20, 1961, and asked me for a little girl. He wanted to name her Randy. I asked him what he thought we needed another baby for and all he could say was that he wanted a little girl and name her Randy. Jack Paar had a little girl named Randy and we used to watch the Jack Paar show all the time. And the way he used to talk about his kid made John want to have a little girl named Randy. I gave her the middle name "Maria" because Johnny Mathis came out with a song "Maria" and whatever Johnny Mathis is, he can sing to me anytime. He soothes me so much that he makes me clean house when I don't want to.

When I became pregnant with Randy, I thought John really wanted her. I didn't know he just wanted another tax exemption. I really thought he wanted that baby, but he's seen that baby maybe ten times in her life and I lived with John until she was eighteen months old. We got orders to come to Plattsburgh, New York, when Randy was about a year old. I was so glad because I knew we'd be closer to home where it would be easier to leave John. He was a very strange man. Maybe his mother didn't hold him enough when he was a baby or maybe he kept hearing her say that she always wanted a girl. He couldn't relate 'cause something was missing in his whole makeup. That's why he made such a good little Fascist. When I see military men, all I see is impotence and egotism. That's what he was. I had a job in a cleaner's in Salina so that I could buy extra bread and milk for my kids because John didn't give me an allowance. He wanted to fly. He wanted to be an officer. The deal was that I would go to nursing school after he got through school. I never went to nursing school while I was with John.

We had to pack up to go to Plattsburgh. And whenever we got transferred, I was the one who was responsible. Most military wives are, but there are some military men who do help their wives. Not all the wives are totally responsible for having the movers come in, and cooking lunch, and driving all over town looking for goddamned car potties and things you don't need if you can go into a motel or hotel when you get tired.

We drove on up to Plattsburgh, New York. This is 1963. When we got into town, of course there was not enough base housing. The same rigamarole. The same bullshit. There was no place for us to live. In fact, in the town of Plattsburgh, there weren't any black people except for a man who owned a rooming house. John had to take me back to New York. I wasn't going to stay with his mother 'cause I wasn't going through that indifference and impersonal bullshit living with her.

I told John to take me to my sister Joleen's

house. And Joleen and I lived in Brooklyn on Cumberland Street in three rooms and the third room was the kitchen which ran into the living room. Actually it was only one big room which all the kids slept in. It was one of them tenements with bedbugs crawling through the goddamned walls. It was hell and it was ugly like anything else in Bedford-Stuyvesant. The kids got dogged up daily. They messed around, got into fights. The neighborhood bullies picked on them. There was always garbage or broken glass to fall on. If you walked in the hall at three or four o'clock in the morning, you would find little kids walking around with no shoes, no clothes, and a bottle of Pepsi-Cola in their hands. We had to stay up till three or four to wait for the milkman to keep the milk from getting stolen. We had eight kids. The bathroom always smelled like dead bodies.

I wrote a letter to John telling him I was going to stay in New York and forget about his ass if he didn't bribe somebody to get us an apartment. Well, between a forty-ounce bottle of Scotch and a twenty-dollar bill we got an apartment on that base in Plattsburgh, New York. We lived next door to a Lieutenant and a Major. The NCO's and airmen had to live on the other side of the base again. I was so glad to have a place of my own. There was a laundry room with a washing machine and dryer. I had an electric stove and a garbage disposal. But the no-food routine, the no-clothes routine set in again.

John and I continued to fight like hell. He used to go down to New York to spend weekends with his friend Theo. Theo was the best man at our wedding and used to write to John regularly. Theo was homosexual. We were home on leave one time and went to a party at his house. I was almost the only straight person there. Anyway, if John could visit Theo I wanted to know why we couldn't go away since we never had a honeymoon. We were never alone with each other in all the years we lived together.

One time when John was in the bullpen, I saw a letter from Theo. I did something I never did in my life: I steamed the letter open and read it. The contents of the letter are as follows:

> *Dear John, You're still in the military. When are you going to get out? I'm tired of seeing you just once a month. I'd like to see you more. So glad you're coming down for the weekend. Don't worry about supper. I'll prepare food for you. Don't worry about wearing any clothes because all we wear is shorts and I'll have some clothes for you to wear. Love always, Theo.*

After I read the letter I was so upset I took it to my priest on base. I told him I was going to leave John because his friendship with Theo was so secretive. This letter symbolized my sicknesses and the impoverished life we had been living. It explained why John was unconcerned about the children and how we were suffering. After my priest read the letter, he told me it was against the laws of the Church for me to leave John.

So I kept trying to hang on, and hang on, but it was over. We had a big argument and we began to fight. I was sitting at the foot of the steps and John snuck up behind me and kicked me in my back. My whole body hit up against the wall. You know, about two years later when I had an X ray at the Navy hospital, the nurse asked me if I had been in an auto accident. I had a rip in my rib cage that looked like it had been cracked and had mended improperly. I still have pains sometimes in my rib cage, sharp pains if I move the wrong way, get up the wrong way. I assume this is where John caught my rib.

    I didn't want to continue like we were living. John said he was going to do what he wanted to do and I could do what I wanted to do. I confronted him with the fact that I was going to get me somebody else to sleep with and he didn't care. But if I had to sleep with somebody else to get along with John, then I didn't need John. So I thought about it and I sat down and said, well hell, if I stay here I could become a junkie, or I could pour liquor in my coffee every morning, and I could sleep around with any man that I want and I could put my kids in a nursery and let them call the lady who runs the nursery "Mama." This went on every day at Plattsburgh. Fuck, that Strategic Air Command has the highest divorce rate and the highest birth rate in the Air Force. They have the highest divorce rate because the husbands are going out of town. They have the highest birth rate because when you're living on a damn SAC base and these damn bombers and fuel planes start up at four o'clock in the morning, you wake up and you got nothing better to do than screw. So most of the babies come from parents being awakened in the morning and having nothing better to do.

There was no reason for me to stay. If I had stayed I would have taken a chance on losing my own self and becoming a junkie and accepting whatever John wanted to dish out. I would have slept around the streets and still remained Captain John's wife. I would have stayed if I could have said he was a good provider, a good father. But he was none of these things. The last time we had a fight, he was locked up in the bedroom. I got out the .45 that he had taught me how to use and I took the safety catch off and I was going to kill him. I had to get away from that. I was getting sick. When we had this fight he beat me up and I called the MP's.

Lt. Salerno came into the house with a brother to assist. They couldn't see the bruises on my body or the big welt that my husband put on my back later on. John was never fighting fair. He wasn't man enough to just stand in front of me and knock the shit out of me. He would get me from the back. I wasn't going to take off my clothes to show those pigs. Lt. Salerno took my husband in the kitchen. I guess they were discussing my "insanity." They wouldn't take John away because he was an officer and an officer is a gentleman by Act of Congress. They take NCO's and airmen away in the truck to the barracks and reprimand them and tell them they are going to get CQ duty, that's doing duty at night in the barracks. But they have to treat John right and they let him drive off base that weekend.

John called me and I said it was all over. After that last argument I couldn't find any reason to stay. I couldn't see staying or my kids staying without being destroyed.

I wanted to see a psychiatrist and the only way you can see a psychiatrist on a military base is if you see a medical doctor first. Then he decides whether or not you need psychiatric care. The doctor had me on Equanil and Stelazine and I was really going out of my mind. I kept begging him to let me see a psychiatrist and he said he couldn't. He said the best thing for me to do, off the record, was to get a boyfriend. He said I shouldn't leave my husband because I didn't have any right to take his kids from him.

So, I went into town while John was on TDY and just randomly picked out a lawyer named Humber. I took Theo's letter with me and I told him what my problem was, how I felt. He said I had grounds for a legal separation. It took attorney Humber two months to get John because of TDY. He had to get a subpoena because John didn't believe I was going. I didn't tell my family because that was my problem and they had their own problems. I had made my bed, now I had to lie in it.

John agreed finally to give me a legal separation and to give the children $300 a month 'cause I got sticky about this matter. Later on, in a second conversation we had, he told me that $250 was for the kids, and the other $50, well, he threw that in for compensation for me. That was very white of him, the black bastard.

7

STU USED to live downstairs in my building in Bayside, Queens, with his sister who was a teacher. I used to watch him from my window all the time because he used to work such erratic hours and I couldn't sleep because I was very hyperactive. I used to look out the window all the time so I couldn't help seeing him. I used to watch this young guy dragging his ass up the walk like he had been workin' in the coal mines. He was in a white uniform all the time and I tried to figure out whether he was an intern or an attendant in a hospital or a medic or something. Come to find out Stu was a manager at Howard Johnson's. His biggest dream was to get enough money together to get a franchise and get his own restaurant. I told him he could forget all about that, honey. He was barking up a blind tree. There aren't too many black men that have franchises in this country and this is why I told him to forget it. The work was so hard. Stu used to work 16 hours a day, sometimes more. He was very earnest in what he was doing.

One day I was taking my youngest for a walk because she wasn't in school then, my youngest child, Randy. Stu was outside and he offered to help me with my bags and then one thing led to another and I helped him clean his car. And the next thing led to another and we began to date. I used to wake

Stu up when it was time for him to go to work. He used to be so tired and the people upstairs used to make so much noise that I used to find Stu curled up in the bathtub in his apartment which was the only quiet place where he could sleep.

He liked to play the marimbas. It's like the xylophone but it has a different sound. Especially when he got mad with me, he played them loud. I could hear from all the way up here on the third floor. That was my signal that he probably wanted to hit me with the batons, but he never did. Stu and I got pretty close. He used to crawl up my steps on his hands and knees, he was so tired. But he'd pass his apartment and come upstairs. His sister hardly ever stayed at the apartment now. She stayed over on Linden Boulevard with one of her friends, so I never saw her. She stayed away to avoid our relationship as well as the noisy neighbors upstairs who kept her from sleeping. She was very religious and me dating Stu was kind of a sacrilege for her. She didn't have much respect for me because she was hung up with some old puritanical bullshit that if you were married or separated, you shouldn't cohabit with males at all. I'm a very healthy female, even though I had had an aversion toward men for some time, and I enjoyed their touch, depending upon who the male is.

I used to lie awake nights waiting for Stu to come home. He used to roll money up underneath my door to wake me up or he'd throw money at my window from way downstairs on the first floor to attract my attention. I used to take care of Stu. I would bathe him and beat life back into him, massaging him. We used to go for walks and rides and he'd sing his favorite song to me, which was "Strangers in the Night." He really thought himself a singer.

One day I was sitting down in his apartment and he was fixing dinner for me. I went to a portfolio that he had and I said, "Stu, who the hell shot these pictures? They're great." He said, "I did." And I was excited because he had shot a picture of a glass of water and a plate with peas and mashed potatoes and roast beef on it and two slices of bread and butter and the way that he shot it, you could almost reach into the picture and touch the food. Then he showed me a lot of pictures of different models and different scenes that he took and I said, "Stu, what the hell are you doing at Howard Johnson's? A black man trying to get a franchise in this country, forget it. You're in the wrong field. Do what you love to do. You're a born photographer."

We were looking through the newspaper one Sunday and I saw a want ad from a company called M——— Incorporated. They had a new process of shooting pictures. They work most with advertising. This process was so new that it wasn't even patented. The stipulation was that if Stu got the job, he would have to master the process of shooting these pictures for the company in thirty days. When Stu was going through all this agony of quitting Howard Johnson's and going down to M———, he and his sister had some beef and he decided that he would come up to my place to stay.

I thought Stu and I would be together for the rest of our lives so I didn't see anything wrong with his coming up.

I couldn't let Stu just go out on the street and I cared very much for him. Plus he always gave me money. He was very fair about that. He was eating my food and if you play, you gotta pay. Everybody got to pay the piper. Stu started working at M——— at outrageous hours and I had a job at a bowling alley as a waitress at night from six to midnight. I needed extra money. I didn't look on Stu to support me or my children. They were my children and I just couldn't stay home when I knew that there were things that they needed. So I got me that job as a waitress and I used to hustle 30 alleys a night with 130 men and I worked hard. They used to call me "small change" cause my name is Penny. I went down to M——— later every night to help Stu shoot pictures 'cause he not only worked eight hours, he stayed there eight more hours. He always had to complete a job. We used to bust our chops. White fellows don't have to do what the black man has to do to prove himself. He has to sweat blood in order to show the master that he is capable of even thinking. To learn this process in thirty days he had to be there on his own time. I felt so much a part of his life.

Possibly I became an object because I made myself an object because I didn't demand a lot of things. I don't mean material things either, because that comes automatically when the person is giving to your emotional needs and sharing with you. Stu and I had been going together for about nine months when I found out I was pregnant. The only way I can tell females to keep from getting pregnant is not to copulate with males. That's the only way. I've had the loop and that's been dislodged. I've had diaphragms and I haven't taken time to put one on and or I have taken it out too soon. This is the only way I can attribute the pregnancy I had with Stu. I pulled the diaphragm out too soon, not thinking. I was afraid to tell him because I knew he wanted his career first. I cared about him; quite naturally I wanted his child.

I finally told him and he said that maybe I could use something. Well, that's the way a man tells you that he doesn't want it. I called up my girl friend and asked her if there was anywhere I could go and get some shots or something. I found that most white doctors will not take the chance. They're not going to ruin their careers for a sister. Most of my white sisters, my counterparts, can afford an abortion where the doctor is willing to take chances or find someone who will take the chance for a certain amount of money. But most white doctors will not take a chance on a black patient. They could give a fuck. My friend found a white doctor for me. He had a shabby office in South Jamaica and all his patients were black. It looked like he hadn't cleaned his damn office in a thousand years, but I guess all he was doing was dispensing pills to help sisters who got pregnant whose men didn't want them have a so-called miscarriage.

I was afraid that John would take the kids if I had a child out of wedlock. I was not divorced from him at the time and he could sue me for immorality because of the "OW" child. "OW" means out of wedlock. That's what courts do to children who are illegitimate. But if Stu had wanted to have that baby I wouldn't have hesitated to have it. If he had said he wanted it because he loved me, I'd have been strong enough to fight John if he tried to take the kids.

I went back to the doctor in that dirty little office after ten days of taking the pills. I was sitting in that miserable, stinking little office with all the miserable little sisters in there, possibly in there for the same reason I was. Most of the time I found that most sisters have abortions because the men don't want them. This doctor was as civilized as he could be. He examined me and he told me that the pregnancy was pretty strong. He put some silver nitrate on a swab which was made of aluminum and he put it all the way up into my cervix and jiggled it around in there. He just kept it up in there for a while and then took it out. He made me lie on the table and told me that if I didn't start bleeding in the next fifteen or twenty minutes, then nothing was going to happen. Nothing did happen and he told me to just go on home and have my baby. So I went home and I was very sad. But I knew that I held pregnancies like a fist.

After I told Stu the series didn't work, his face dropped to the floor. I saw the hurt in his face and the sadness. I asked him if he wanted the baby and he looked up at me as if he had never known me before, as if we never had nothing. He said "no." I took a bottle of Scotch and threw it at him and missed his head by about two inches. I called up my girl friend again and asked her if she knew anybody else. She did. I made an appointment with with him and it was supposed to be like a normal examination. By that time I was about eight weeks' pregnant and I could feel the fetus in me. If you feel for the fetus, you feel the knot in your uterus. You know it's there, never mind the kicking.

The doctor asked me the history of everything that was wrong with me. I asked him why I suffered from cystitis so bad, why I had so many cysts and staph infections when I was with my husband. And he told me that either my husband was packing shit or sleeping with whores. I guess he could tell me that because he wasn't in the military. He's a private doctor and a brother. He asked me why I wanted to abort the child and I told him how Stu said he didn't want it and it seemed like all the love I had for Stu just drained out of me from the time he said so. Just seeing him repulsed me. I wanted to scratch his eyes out because that baby was just as much a part of him as me. Father means life-giver as far as I'm concerned and Stu put life into that egg that was inside of me. He didn't want that baby and it hurt me so bad. It was like he abandoned me.

I also told the doctor that I was afraid I was going to lose my children. He said he didn't want to tamper with the pregnancy because he knew I really wanted the child. He knew friends in the military and lawyers and decided to look into whether or not I would lose the children. The doctor said he would discuss the abortion with me after that. About three or four days later he called me up and told me that I had another appointment with him. When I got into his office he looked so sad. I knew what his answer was going to be. He had spoken to his military friends and lawyers and found out that if I had the child I stood a one hundred percent chance of losing all the children if my husband decided to take me to court.

He sent me to this woman who was a registered nurse. She was very kind, like the doctor. They didn't make me feel dirty. In a way I wanted it to be a back-street thing and I wanted to really, really suffer because I knew I was doing something against my own personal principles that I had set up for me. I'm not talking for every woman because each woman is an individual with the right to decide whether she wants to be a mother or not, 'cause it means thirty to forty years of her life and after that struggle, the children are still coming home. So I'm speaking of me personally. The doctor told me that the abortion would be $150 and I was to give the money to the woman. You know that doctor wasn't running an abortion mill to make money.

I called up Stu on his job 'cause at this point Stu had found a place of his own to live. I told him I needed $150. I took the kids out to my girl friend's on Long Island and Stu picked me up. I don't know where he got the money from and I don't give a fuck where he got the money from. But he had it in a white envelope. We went to the woman's house. Normally it takes a few seconds to insert a rectal tube up into the cervix. It took her twenty-five minutes to insert it into my cervix because I have a floating uterus. Once the tube is placed, you start bleeding and it's the type of blood, the brightest, reddest blood I've ever seen. I was laying up in that woman's bedroom with my legs up in the air and all I could see was my child's life slipping away from me. I just hated Stu 'cause he was a punk. He didn't have no balls 'cause if he had loved me and stood up beside me even if I had lost my kids, I would have had him and that baby. All these thoughts were going on in my head and Bill was sitting out in that woman's living room waiting, having a drink.

The fetus is supposed to die once you start losing blood. When the tube stays up there for about twenty-four hours it will expel on its own and the fetus should expel when the tube slips out. I felt so terrible but I even felt like I didn't have a right to cry. I wanted to die because I was doing something that I didn't want to do 'cause I wanted that baby. When I got back home I mopped floors. My parents happened to come by and visit me that day and I think it was because whenever my father didn't hear from me, he came by. I think he knew what was going on but he didn't say anything. Maybe he picked up the odor of the blood which was very distinct. I don't care how clean you are, you can't scrub away the odor of the blood that comes from you when you have an abortion. He also knows me very well.

That night I went on down to the city to help Stu shoot pictures. Every time I went to the bathroom, I could see the tube sticking right out of my vagina and the blood was coming through the center of it. Every time I went to the bathroom I'd just see my life going down the toilet. By the time we got back home, I was bleeding very profusely. It was snowing and I got scared 'cause I didn't think I could get back to the nurse 'cause I was supposed to go back to her the next day. When I went to the bathroom about three o'clock that morning, I saw that the tube had come out too soon. It didn't stay up there for twenty-four hours. Stu ran downstairs to get Gertrude, my friend. Gertrude is a nurse and she had a baby around the same time I would have if I didn't have an abortion. She named that baby "Penny" and whenever I see that child I remember that I am supposed to have one the same age. Gertrude gave me a vaginal and she pushed and pushed and I kept losing blood, blood, blood all over the place. I was in so much pain and the fetus wouldn't come out. Gertrude couldn't feel it. After she tried to squeeze as much blood out of me as she could, I told her to go downstairs. This was very traumatic for her since she was pregnant herself.

I was getting a temperature and I got hot one moment and had cold flashes another and I still felt something up inside of me. Stu and I took almost two hours to get back to the nurse's house and I was so afraid that I was going to develop an infection or something. I didn't want to have to go that far and die 'cause the reason I was having the abortion was so I could keep my kids. At that time I was saying to myself it would serve me right.

When we got to the woman's house she examined me. The fetus had died up inside of me and it couldn't be expelled even with a tube up there and all that bleeding. It should have slipped right out. We had to go back to the doctor's office. I didn't get prepped; my pubic hair wasn't shaved. There's no such thing as sterile conditions. You do what you have to do. I was immediately put on the table and my feet put up in the stirrups. The nurse strapped my wrists down and stayed with me all the time.

I saw the doctor come out with the scrapers that they use for D&C's. She had to put me in a local anesthesia, most likely it was Demerol. But I couldn't be knocked out. The doctor dilated me, which is very painful. I felt and heard every scrape that the D&C instrument made. It hurt so bad I almost went insane. Can you imagine going through a D&C under local anesthesia when they put you out in a hospital? They're scraping away what's up in the uterus and the walls hurt so, so bad.

And all the nurse kept saying, patting me, was, "Harrisene, Harrisene, don't holler now. The cleaning man is outside. You don't want to get the doctor in trouble. Harrisene, Harrisene." This is the only thing that kept me sane, her calling my name, patting my arm. She kept giving me a little bit more Demerol and when that would wear off, she would give me a little bit more. I wanted to scream and all I could think about was Stu sitting out in the outside of the goddamned office. I just wanted to kill him.

After the doctor was finished, I saw him leave me and I saw him take an emesis basin which is a kidney-shaped pan that they give you in the hospital to brush your teeth. I wondered where he was taking my baby. Now wasn't that insane? Knowing that the baby was in that little basin, I was wondering where he was taking my baby. I knew where he was taking it. He was taking it to flush it down the goddamned toilet. It couldn't have been no bigger than my fist.

The nurse helped me off the table and the next thing I knew the doctor disappeared. She told me that I had to walk up those steps from the doctor's office, which was down in the basement, by myself. I was so groggy and I thought she was crazy after she said that. But she disappeared. Everything was like it had never happened and she must have told Stu that he couldn't help me outside the door. My main concern was for the doctor. He did the D&C and didn't get shit for it. He looked into my case to see if I would lose the kids. He couldn't give me blood or antibiotics but he gave me a tremendous amount of iron pills. The man jeopardized his career for me. On top of that, he made me come back for a check-up six weeks later. He didn't just dump me in the street and say go for yourself. He followed me through and goddamn it, I was so strong that I didn't have any setbacks. So I walked through all that snow, all the way up the block to Stu's car. He couldn't help me because we couldn't put any suspicion on what was going on.

From then on, for about three or four weeks, I used to wake up in cold sweats and hear my baby crying. And one day I was walking down the street and I was crying and didn't know I was. That is how the abortion affected me emotionally. But Cor saw that I was crying.

I didn't have any infection, I didn't have any setbacks. Immediately after the abortion, I went and got the kids. It was the same day that I got the D&C. The lady that put the tube up there called me a couple of times. I think she wanted to be my friend. But I didn't want her to be my friend. I didn't need any reminders. Even after I had the abortion, Stu still wanted us to go on and have a relationship. That really took a lot of balls to think that after he didn't want the baby and saw me go through all that hell. He came telling me about how he didn't realize how much I loved him.

I got so strong that I went back to work. I was strong enough to knock the shit out of Stu. But there I was minus a baby. Stu stayed with me on and off. He mastered the special process at M——— and became the head photographer. It took me three or four months though to get out of my depression. In the meantime I still had the children to deal with and I still had the desire to go back to school.

I had to wait until I got a missive from my stepmother. Usually when I slack up or get too depressed, or like I'm not doing anything, she tells me off in a loving way. She told me to get up off my ass and go out there and feed my niggers. I think the day after I received that letter from her, I went to Creedmore and applied for a psychiatric attendant position. That was in 1966. I was still full of most of the ideals I had when I was a youngster. I wanted to help people and I felt that through Creedmore, I could eventually go into nursing.

I didn't know it was pretty difficult to become a

nurse by working at Creedmore. And working at Creedmore just dampened my whole everything. I almost stopped wanting to be a nurse because of the things that I saw there. And I was reminded of the abortion. I was sitting in one of the classes and they were teaching us how to give simple soap enemas. The nurse pulled out a rectal tube and an emesis basin and I almost fainted. It brought back all those memories again.

8

I MET Marketa Kimbrell in 1968. I had just gotten off duty at Creedmore State Hospital and was preparing dinner for my crumbsnatchers. There was a knock at my door. Two women working for the Women's Strike for Peace were asking for petitions to be signed against the war in Vietnam. Of course I signed the petition. I told Marketa (one of the women) that I was the wife of a flyer and had lived on SAC (Strategic Air Command) bases for almost six years and that the war in Vietnam concerned me and my children.

Marketa asked me if I would petition with her. She is a blonde with a foreign accent and found it difficult at times canvassing. With both of us together, one black and one blonde working a common cause, we might get more signatures. At that time being against the war was not very popular. We exchanged telephone numbers. That's when I still had a telephone.

The very next evening Marketa came to my house and we ventured out together from door to door. We weren't always successful since most people were apprehensive about discussing the war pro or con. But there were some people who were brave enough to sign the petition stating that we should get the hell out of Vietnam!

Marketa and I became very close. She made me

become aware. I began to go to peace marches and see for myself just what was happening as far as social issues were concerned. Marketa worried about my getting hurt at rallies. She told me that I had to stay loose and in good health because of my children. But she put her life on the line on CORE picket lines, grape pickers lines and many other causes.

With her friend Richard Levy, Marketa was getting an acting group together called the City Street Theater. One day she asked me if I wanted to join it and work with her group and do some poetry.

I said, "I don't want to do any poetry. What do I know about poetry?"

Marketa had faith in me as a person and said that I had a natural ability to act. I laughed and I said, "Didn't you know that all black folks are actors? We've been acting for four hundred years."

Our group consisted of everyday people from the streets. We worked hard together as one and we created a beautiful show called "An Evening with Lorca." I worked five days a week, weekends, and holidays. The performances were scheduled every day I worked. I came from Queens on the subways and buses with the children. It was a hassle but I did it because I was committed. When people create, it's like raising a child, shaping it, crying and feeling pain and despair over it and then one day it makes its debut, its first performance to the world and then you find you did well.

Richard Levy made me aware of my natural beauty. It was he who told me to wear my hair natural. One day he said to me, "Penny, why do you press your hair? Don't you know how beautiful black women are? And I said, "Who, me, wear my hair nappy? Not me!" But I went home one evening after work, washed my hair, and never pressed it again. To revert was very new for me and I had to learn how to comb and care for my hair, learn how to lift the curls with a pick. It was like caring for a garden. After that I began to wear my "freedom" with pride. To me it wasn't an "Afro"—it was my freedom. I was unchained from the pressing comb and the torture I was putting myself through because I thought it was the thing to do. I had been trying to look like my white sisters because I had been programmed all my life to think that black was ugly, that nappy was ugly. It sure was insane of me to press out the curl to get my hair straight and to press the curl back in with hot curling irons. And it took a white man to tell me about getting my hair together.

Anyway, our rehearsals were vigorous. We rehearsed for the show everywhere and anywhere. During one of our rehearsals at the Cooper Square Theater, a little store on Cooper Square, I met a friend of Marketa's, Beatrice Blau. It was through Beatrice that I met my dear, sweet, sensitive friend, Leo Hamalian. After my episode at City (see Leo's introduction) I almost didn't meet him. We discussed the Seek Program and found out that I didn't qualify for it because I wasn't living in a "poverty area." My family was living off $3,600 a year but I was penalized because some dudes got together and drew some boundary lines and defined poverty stricken areas. I've worked three jobs at once so that my kids wouldn't have to live in Harlem or South Jamaica. My kids aren't street people and they would never survive.

Somehow things got worked out. It's September, 1968, and I'm ready to go to school.

I'm working at Harcourt, Brace & World as an editorial trainee. My friend Lyn Dobrin is babysitting for me. I managed to get up almost $300 to start classes. I'm going to school three nights a week. I have three kids, Cor, Jennings, and Randy, in school now but then the school strike comes. I was able to cope with that one week but the next week that they struck I had to stop work.

Cor, my oldest child, was beginning to show signs of being disturbed. She was put on medication and nobody would take the responsibility of giving her the medication, because she would go through big changes. She'd spit it up or get very paranoid about it, which was to be understood. So I had to go home. I resented this because my job at Harcourt, Brace was the first sit-down job I ever had. My feet swelled from inactivity but I was able to use my mind. And the people were so lovely. The hardest thing about working was fighting those damn subways. Garcia Lorca called them the "blood trains with manacled roses." The hardest part was that rush hour going to work and the rush hour coming home. Even though I only made $89 a week after they took the taxes out, it didn't matter. I was functioning and had a little money to buy a pair of shoes or a little bread. But you have to come home. There's nothing you can do about it.

About two weeks before I left Harcourt, Brace,

as I was walking down the street to work, I saw a very attractive elderly man passing me. I remember thinking to myself that he was very good-looking for an old man. A split second after I thought this he was right next to me. And he was so full of it. He said to me, "If I promise not to walk too fast, can I walk along with you?" So I said, "I don't mind," because I still had that thought in my mind how handsome this elderly man was.

The first thing he told me was that my Afro was beautiful. I remember telling him my hair wasn't no Afro. They're making Afros outa synthetic plastic. I told him my hair was freedom. I wear my hair like this because I'm free enough and bold enough to dig myself the way I am. If anybody's going to like me, he's going to like me for what I am. René pardoned himself. We walked and talked from the corner of West 57th Street all the way to the 7th Avenue subway. It was like we'd known each other in another world. I was completely and totally consumed by René's presence. And we kissed goodbye at the subway, just a friendly little peck. And I was surprised at myself because I had had adverse feelings about men for quite a while. I really hadn't been interested in getting involved with a man since 1964, 1965. René gave me his home address and his home telephone number, and his job number, and he told me he was a public relations man. And I never knew what a public relations man was. After meeting René, I assumed that if you were good at bullshit, you could be a PR man or woman.

By the time I got to Harcourt, Brace & World

that afternoon, the secretary at the front desk told me there was a telephone call for me. I picked up my phone and it was René. He asked me if he could take me to lunch. And I let him take me to lunch. I waited for him and he jumped out of a cab at lunchtime. I took a two-hour lunch that day and didn't anybody miss me.

All the way home that day I was just as happy as a bluebird. Very happy. The children were home by the time I got home. We usually went shopping on Friday nights for groceries for the week. We'd pull 'em up the hill and go to a movie that night, the late movie. Sometimes I'd take the kids down to 42nd Street. I don't take 'em down there anymore because of all the shooting up and prostitution going on. That night, which was a Friday night, my phone rang just before I went shopping. And it was René himself. And I said to myself, "Wow, this dude, he sure don't ever quit do he?" He asked me could he come spend the evening with me and my children and I told him "Yep." I told him I had to go shopping and I gave him the address and directions as best I could. By the time we got back up the hill with the groceries, René was sittin' outside in his car. And I was glad to see him because I had just pulled those groceries up hard-trouble hill, which I call the "bitch." He helped me bring the groceries up to the third floor.

We went to the drive-in movie that night. We had a nice time. By the time we got home it was about three A.M. I told René that he might as well sack himself here. There was no sense in trying to drive back to the city that night. Well, René never left that weekend. All he did was listen to me gab. He met my parents because they were spending a lot of weekends with me at that time. They babysat for me and we went out. I was so forward. It was the first time I ever went to a motel just to screw! I thought because René was older than me he was gonna be light stuff. Well, he sure did fool me.

I talked to René on the telephone every day. If I couldn't hear his voice I was lost. He would pick me up every night from school. I just fell head over heels in love with him. We didn't have much of a courtship. Somehow the twenty-two years difference in our age did away with the kidding. Also, I was a very serious woman at the age of twenty-seven. We didn't have to kid like you take me out to dinner and you come over and meet the parents and we hold hands and we walk a while and then we decide we're going to sleep together. René knew that I wanted him and I knew that he wanted me. That's not being loose. That's just being positive and realistic.

I wasn't living with René. If a man doesn't live in the same house with you and you don't see his underwear and you don't see the extra toothbrush and you don't see the razors and the shaving lotion, you are more inclined to forget your birth control pills. My period didn't come and I missed my period five times in my life and I have four children to show for those five times. I didn't tell René I was pregnant because he was on his way to India. He just said that he had to get away so he hopped a ship with a strong heartbeat of a twenty-one year old man. He was up on the masts painting them and I felt like if this is what he wanted to do, I didn't want to stand in his way. I figured if I told him I was pregnant before he left, he might not have made the trip and gotten away like he wanted to.

But life has a way; we don't have any control over our destiny sometimes. René hadn't been out to sea for more than five weeks when he broke his foot. One of the other seamen dropped a hatchet on his foot. René had to be flown back to the United States with his foot in a cast. The first thing that I said to him was that I was pregnant and he'd better not say a goddamned thing. He said an abortion was the furthest thing from his mind. He was very tender, in fact. He was very patient and very loving and he didn't hide me. We walked all over Harlem together. René's the type of man that is always getting stopped and greeted. We'd walk down 125th Street and even the junkies would say hello. René Jaques got to be some kind of all right.

When I was about five months' pregnant, I had to give Cor a spanking. She used to walk up and down the hall in our two-by-four apartment and stop outside my bedroom. She would say that she hoped the baby was born deformed. She wanted to know why I wan't having an abortion. I felt like she was trying to run me crazy. I got up and beat her with a strap. I beat her so bad that she bled. The strap bit into her flesh. I didn't want to do it but I didn't know what else to do. After I spanked her she told me she was going to die. Randy and Jennings put peroxide and cold water on her. Jennings tried to tell her that she shouldn't say things like that to Mommy because the new baby is their brother or sister and it's growing inside the same stomach that they grew in.

This reminded me of how happy Jennings was when he was only three and I was pregnant with Randy. We were living in Kansas. The bread man came to the door and Jennings pulled the bread man's coat and saying that he could leave three loaves of bread today because Mommy's having a baby and it's growing like a flower inside her stomach. This is the kind of kid he was, which explains the way he was trying to talk to Cor the day I spanked her. It wasn't a spanking, it was a beating. I didn't send her to school for ten days, because if anyone had seen the welts on her, they probably would have put me in jail.

Cor needed me at home and I came home. I didn't want to leave Harcourt but I did. But Cor thought her medication was poison and I had to pretend I was taking the same medicine so that she would take it. I went down to welfare and asked them to supplement my income because I had to come home to a child who was emotionally and mentally disturbed. She was being treated at Queens Hospital and was deteriorating. When I was working eight hours a day and going to school three nights a week, everything went to pot. Jennings would have been locked outside the door. I'd come home at midnight and find him sleeping on the steps. I wanted to get an education so that I could have a profession, but if you have a disturbed child, you have no business working.

The welfare office in Long Island City is in a big

loft building. It's ugly and no wonder the investigators and the social workers and the clerks are so nasty to people who come for help. Anybody who can go through the dehumanization that you go through down there to get your goddamn tax dollar back deserves welfare even if they're lying. Whenever I go to welfare, I've never felt like I was getting handouts 'cause I'm a taxpayer. My father's been working for over forty years and whatever tax dollar is down there is mine 'cause my father will drop dead before he'll live to benefit from any kind of welfare payments.

Like my friend Clary says, if you're white all you have to do is tell 'em your husband is a hippie and any old kinda thing you call him and you can get welfare right away. The black sister goes down there and catches hell. They can deal with sisters coming down there and telling them that either their husbands are dead or junkies. They want you to wallow in the street. They want you to go down there and tell them your husband is a junkie, that you have four or five kids and all of them have different fathers. You see, they can deal with that shit. If they find you in the gutter, they can say they pulled you up by the bootstraps.

So my going down there and tellin' them my husband was a professional and an officer in the Air Force and I was receiving $300 a month support money and the fact that my rent was $150 didn't faze them. They couldn't deal with it. So they came to my house with all these bullshit questions about what I'm doing with a telephone. I went down to welfare three, four, five times before

I got any help. I was afraid to tell them I was pregnant. I didn't have the strength to go to court with a belly asking for an increase.

I called up my friend Leo and asked him if he could get a scholarship for Cor to go to camp. I couldn't have her in the house when I had the baby. Leo called me back and said he got a scholarship for her, but I was to write to the director and ask him if he would take the responsibility of giving Cor the medication twice a day. She was still on tranquilizers. They wrote back to me and I gave them a history of Cor's illness. They agreed to take her and I know the only reason why they agreed to take her was because of Leo. I found out it's who you know. The last thing Cor asked me before she left for camp was to let her know when the baby was born. I guess the people at the camp coped well with her. There's a difference when more than one person deals with personality, especially when that personality is becoming dislocated.

Immediately after Cor left for camp, Jennings, who is a worrywart like me, got a job at a gas station owned by Sid, my friend June's husband. My friend June, by the way, bought all of Cor's clothes for camp. Jennings was ten years old; he worked five days a week and used to come home so greasy and I know he used to work hard because he would fall through the door, too tired to eat, and would go straight to the shower. It ain't any time Jennings would take a bath every day. This brings up another episode about Jennings: He got the job so that he could save his money; he got paid $22 a week and Sid used to buy his lunch every day, but you know what he did? He used to pay Sid back for buying his lunch because he said he didn't want nobody buyin' him nothin'. He had his little pride and it wasn't false. He just didn't want any handouts and he worked hard pumping gas, counting change, and working the customer's credit cards and everything. Jennings saved up all his money and one day he was so tired that he was draggin' himself out of the house that morning and I came down with my big belly and I said, "What's the matter, Jennings?" He said, "Mommy, I'm so tired!" with tears in his eyes—ten years old! And I said, "Well, you don't have to go to work today," and he cried and said, "But if I don't go to work I won't get paid." And it just ripped my heart open for him to feel so responsible for my responsibility, because he wanted to go to camp and knew the only way he could go and the only way he could free me from worrying was to work in that gas station.

So there I was, Cor was in camp, Jennings working, my pregnancy coming to its end, and me on my last lap. René and I had lots of arguments, we tiffed a lot. I don't know whether it was because I was eight months' pregnant, hot and raggedy, and poorly dressed. I've never been a person that valued clothes or material things, but you know how bad you feel when you're pregnant especially if you was as big as I was. I looked deformed, I did.

We named the baby after Lamumba Abdul Shakur, one of the Panther 21. We had met Lamumba and Afeni Shakur, and all the Panthers before the

21 bust. When they were picked up in my six months' pregnancy, I was so upset about it that I said, "If I could have twenty-one babies I'd name every last one of them after the brothers and sisters that were busted on so-called conspiracy charges." René got word to Lamumba Abdul Shakur that if we were to have a son, he would be named after him. That really gave Lamumba Abdul his cookies.

Gertrude got very nervous when she was checking Lumumba out 'cause he had a growth on his hand and she thought he only had two fingers. The doctor tied the big round bubble off and Lumumba was all right. When René came up to see the baby, he caused all this commotion. René was up there cussin' the nurse, tellin' her he wanted to see the Jaques baby. But I was on Medicaid there and since my name wasn't Jaques the baby's name wasn't Jaques. But René was lookin' for the "Jaques" baby. Since we weren't hiding Lamumba, I didn't clock in at the hospital as a "Jaques." And I wasn't waiting around to find out if he could afford it or not, especially since we weren't getting along too well. When he finally saw the baby, he was so thrilled that he came to the hospital every day. He had no concept of how long he could stay. He stayed as long as he felt like it.

So Lamumba's full name is Lamumba Shakur Jaques. Lamumba Shakur is for Lamumba Abdul Shakur who took his name from Patrice Lamumba, the revolutionary and liberator in the Belgian Congo who was murdered and buried in an unmarked grave, and "Jaques" for René. It sounds sort of contradictory but that's where it's at. We are Africans, we do come from Africa, and Jaques did have a lot of slaves.

I took little Lamumba to the courtroom to see big Lamumba Abdul and to watch the hypocrisy and injustices that went on in that courtroom. Afeni was to get to hold Lamumba at the May 4 rally when she got out on bail. I marched five miles with my friend Orgy, and another one of my friends, and took that baby on my back all the way. Afeni had Lamumba up on stage with her. She tried to hold the baby up because we were by Long Island City prison where Lamumba Abdul was. The cops let him come out on the catwalk and said, "Hey, there's a kid out there that your wife got named after you." But he couldn't get a good look at the baby and told me to keep bringing him to court so he could see him growing and developing. In July of 1971, Lamumba Abdul Shakur just got out of jail on other charges besides the charges he was acquitted of with the 21.

My stay at the hospital was all right this time. I breast-fed Lamumba. Medicaid makes you stay five days so the hospital can at least get more than they would have, just for putting up with your Medicaid behind. Gertrude used to come see me every night when she got off work at eleven. I had to get the heat lamp for my stitches because I knew I had to heal fast. I knew what I had to face when I got home. So I had to take a lot of baths and I had to bake my potatoes. That's what I call putting the heat lamp on the episiotomy, bakin' your potatoes. It draws the pain out and dries the area fast.

I had Lamumba the day before his sister Randy was to turn seven. Jennings was so excited he tried to come up to the hospital and sneak in. But he wasn't old enough to get through. We tried to slip him off as twelve, but the age was fourteen. But I peeked out through the window and he was dressed up so fine in his fancy street clothes which he had worked for and paid for. He had cigars in his pocket. He was so proud.

René came to pick me up from the hospital on the fifth day. That was the slowest ride home I ever had. May I never feel it when I die and have a funeral. That car went as slow as a hearse. René didn't want no flies to light on Lamumba. When we got home all my friends were waiting for us . . . June, Cal, Scott, Antie, everybody. Jennings was so happy he was crying. He was so happy he had a brother and that I was all right. But I wasn't in the door two minutes when I saw on the table the mail saying that my husband was instituting action against me. He didn't say what he was suing me for. He just said that I should look for a subpoena in the mail, or whatever that was. So, I got real scared.

9

My first, biggest concern was Coretta. You know, it's ironic, but the same day I came home from the hospital, Cor had asked the director of the YMCA camp if she could talk to me to see if I had the baby. Coretta woke me up and I told her that I had the baby. I didn't know how I was going to be able to tell her. Fate just worked out so well. Our communications were right. We had a little mental telepathy going there. I told her she had a brother and she was very happy. She was very, very happy, the other Cor. There were two Cors. The Cor we call Corry was very happy that Lamumba was born. But the other Cor was surfacing.

There were too many people pulling from me. And there were too many things I had to set straight. My relationship with René was deteriorating. I had another child. John was facing me with the threat that I might lose my children. But I just commenced to fall right into the program. I was scrubbin' floors, handwashing eighty-five diapers every two days, breast-feeding the baby and taking care of him and my other two children who were home.

The day after I came home from the hospital I was on my way down the hill to take Lamumba to the doctor. He had to have some sutures removed from his penis. When they first brought Lamumba to me in the hospital, I undressed him, like I undressed all my babies when I saw them for the first time, to see what's what. I remember him having gauze over the circumcision. The machine they used to circumsize Lamumba got jammed and the foreskin on Lamumba's penis was hit too far. Gertrude told me not to worry about the surgery they would have to do. I wasn't worried about the surgery, I didn't want any problems with my grandchildren, that's what I was worried about. Dr. Arbib made sure he was all right.

There was no time for rest. Leo got another scholarship for two weeks in camp, but for Jennings. He was still workin' the gas station, and he had saved up all his little money making $22 a week. Jennings bought all the things he needed for camp. But before he left for camp, we had some problems with the disturbed mother downstairs. The first time I had had a confrontation with her I was working for Harcourt, Brace & World. Coretta called me up on the telephone and she was hysterical. I heard all this bangin' on the door through the telephone. I asked Coretta to control herself and tell me what was wrong. Mrs. Wright from downstairs was bangin' on my door. I got very upset and called René to tell him I was cutting my classes that night and ask him to drive me home because this woman was terrorizing my children. Nobody knew that Coretta was extra, extra sensitive about being screamed at. She'd get hysterical, it was part of her disturbance.

I came home, fed the children, sat them down to do their homework, and went downstairs. I did not use any four-letter words, which is what she expected from me. I simply told her that I was the mother of Coretta and Jennings and that she was terrorizing them. I asked her not to come up to the third floor again and if she had any problems, she was to leave me a note in my mailbox or stop me on my way into the house. She claimed she didn't know I worked but she lived in a front apartment and saw me leave every day. I explained to her that black folk work six days a week, from sunup to sundown, but that went over her head. I told her not to bring her posterior region up to the third floor to dispense any type of discipline because of any petty differences between children, which are petty since they'll be friends tomorrow. After this, the woman harassed my children daily. One day I found her refereeing a fight between my youngest daughter and her son. "Go on Jimmy, kill her, kill her." Now, that was sick.

A week before Jennings went to camp, and Lamumba wasn't quite ten days old, I was washing diapers in the sink. I had just got through scrubbing the floors and my episiotomy was giving me pain. My milk wasn't coming down too well because I was having lots of emotional strain. On this particular day I was to lose my milk. I looked out the window and there was Mrs. Wright screaming in my ten-year-old's face like she was a maniac.

Jennings was taking care of Ollie and Rosie McNamara's kids for me because I was babysitting for them. Jimmy, Mrs. Wright's son, hit the little two-year-old boy, Cyril, and Jennings had the older brother, who was four, fight Jimmy, who was eight, back. So Mrs. Wright took it on herself to harass Jennings. I screamed out the window and called her ten kinds o' bitches. She cursed me upstairs, called me all kinds of whores and niggers, which just rolled off my back. I told myself I couldn't go down there because she didn't put a hand on Jennings. I knew she was insane and I told myself to leave her be. I wanted to go downstairs and shake her but I repressed it so much that when I came into the dining room I passed out from pain in my kidney region. My body wasn't healed.

I had to sit down for a while. Then I went back into the kitchen and I was washing diapers. I heard her scream through my window, "Bitch, I'm gonna kill 'em." And I couldn't believe it. I looked out the window and she told me what she was going to do. She ran down the walk and physically attacked my son. She was hitting him in his chest and arms. Jennings immediately went into an attack stance and gave her a bad kick in the face. I had put Jennings in karate school right after the Wallace rally to teach him to protect himself and have the heart to relate normally to an abnormal dialogue.

The only thing that I saw was red. Any mother sees red when her child is attacked by anything. I ran down three flights of stairs and I jumped on her. I wanted to kill her. And she pulled my hair, and I told her, "You see, it's not hard, it's not like Brillo. It's very soft and it's very beautiful but it's strong and you can't hurt it." And then she called me a nigger and I punched her in the mouth. I gave her a punch for my mother, who died an exslave. I tried to pulverize this woman who thought my son was little nigger. It took two, big strong men to pull me off her. I saw the hate in Jennings' eyes and in his body and he was crying because he didn't want his mommy to get hurt. But all pain disappeared from my body. But when I sat down to breast-feed Lamumba, I discovered that I had no more milk.

The next day I went down on the subway to Long Island City and got me a summons for child harassment. I served it on her the same day. I knew she would show up because she thought the laws that are written are there to keep me and my people in our places. She appeared in court and read off of a piece of paper her lies. This was after I told the judge why I took out the summons. She claimed that my son attacked her and her two boys and she looked like the Southern belle that was degraded by a big black bitch. The judge was looking for this vicious black son of mine and realized that this ten-year-old kid that was standin' next to me was the attacker. That was the beginning of Jennings' indoctrination into the proceedings of the courtroom.

This episode could have destroyed my son. I was afraid he would dislike all white women. I didn't know how Jennings felt. Usually, he draws pictures to get out his hostility. When Martin Luther King was murdered Jennings watched the funeral on television. The other children took it in stride but Jennings broke out crying. That night he drew a picture of fire billowing out of a building, and people trying to get out the windows, and downstairs there was a fire engine with water that was reachin' them. I related the water with hope but the fire with hostility. He also drew a picture of a bomber with fire coming out of the sky and the plane was goin' toward water to extinguish the fire. Jennings is sensitive. When the commercial would come on of the kids from Biafra, Jennings used to cry and wanted to give the little money he had to those hungry people. And he'd say, "We have so much here, why can't we give?" So Jennings knew Mrs. Wright was just one rotten apple in the bunch.

WHEN Lamumba was six weeks old, I had to meet Cor at the bus terminal after she had spent six weeks in camp. That was the next big trauma. At first, because Lamumba was so tiny, she didn't want to deal with him. And I didn't want to make her hold him. Eventually she said she'd hold him. She was very protective toward him, but it was over-protective. I told her she didn't have to play the mother role. Mrs. Rosen, the social worker I had been seeing at Queens Hospital, told me to be very careful with Coretta and the baby because Cor might hurt the child. When I was pregnant with Lamumba, Cor kept insisting that I have an abortion. She used to tell me the least René could do was marry me.

It took me a long time to believe what Mrs. Rosen said. The first time I saw this white broad sitting behind the desk, I said to myself, "What the hell can she tell me." So I walked into her office very hostile, with my façade goin', you know, Miss Pillar of Strength. I guess I scared her to death.

Here I was with this big, abnormal-sized belly and this bushy head, and I come in there with my lip hangin' out 'cause I know this broad can't tell me nothing 'cause she's white and middle class, right? I had been very hostile toward Mrs. Rosen for about three visits until one day I decided to listen and not talk. The phone rang on her desk, and it kept ringing. Each of the calls was from kids. I heard her explain to the kids, "No, Johnny can't take his bike out today. Wait till I come home in an hour and I'm gonna cook so and so." Damn her whiteness, damn the middle-class whiteness or the social worker attitude. I realized that we could be relating as mothers and that's when I let go that façade and I let her help me.

It's a bitch. I've been confronted by a thousand social workers. Most of them have preconceived ideas about blacks and about poor people. They all think poor people are nasty and dirty and want to be poor. Their biggest desire is to be poor. But somebody had to help me so that I could help Cor. Somebody had to do it and Mrs. Rosen was willing. We finally met on the same grounds. All I can remember her sayin' was protect the baby. Can you understand what it feels like to have to protect a baby from another child that comes from the same womb?

I went to work when Lamumba was three weeks old. I got a very good job with Manpower. It was workin' for a poverty program called "The Originals, Inc." in South Jamaica. I was really supposed to have a car but since I was making $150 a week I assumed I could get one. My girl friend Carlotta baby-sat for me and only charged $12 a week. Takin' care of Lamumba was worth more than $12 a week, but those are the kinds of friends I have. But Lamumba got very sick with bronchitis and I just had to stop working. My boss called me for three weeks and asked me to come back. But I had to stay home with my baby.

Lamumba had 105° temperature and I knew if he didn't see a doctor, he was gonna die. It was snowing and I had no car and I was supposed to make meetings at the local school to discuss what federal and state grants it was entitled to. And I felt bad 'cause I had a good job and I was makin' good money. So I took Lamumba down the hill looking for a doctor. But all the doctors would say, "You Medicaid? I don't take it." You know doctors are supposed to be humane, but it's money they're after. Humanistic doctors are few and far between.

I walked way down the block and I saw this big house that had doctors' signs outside and I thought it looked too ritzy. But I walked into the office anyway and it was crowded the way it always is. A strong, handsome doctor came out. He must've been in the sun, his skin was so brown. I walked into the office and I had tears streaming down my face and I told him my baby was sick and my baby was going to die and all I had was Medicaid. I didn't have no money. Dr. Martin walked over to me and took my baby from me and said, "I take Medicaid, don't you worry. Give me your baby." And Lamumba has been seeing Dr. Martin ever since and I know it costs him more money to hire a secretary to fill out all those forms.

Dr. Martin is the only doctor besides Dr. Arbib who really cared. I don't care how much it costs them to go to med school. It still doesn't take the place of humanism which is what we're talking about when we talk about the kids in Harlem and in the streets. But Dr. Martin knew that Lamumba was named after a very special man. And Dr. Martin and his brother are the only doctors who make house calls. We got a lot of old people here and they ain't got no business on that hill. It's just too much for them; in fact, it's almost too much for me.

This was in September, 1969. Cor was deteriorating very rapidly. Then Lamumba got better and I was to apply again for a job at Creedmore. I never thought I'd go back to Creedmore, never thought I would. But I knew I couldn't stay home. I had to supplement my income. I had another child. I had no choice. He had to eat. And in this world, and especially in this country, if you don't work, you don't eat. No money, no food. That's where it's at.

I had quit my job at Creedmore a year before this but I knew that they would rehire me. I was a qualified poo-poo cleaner. We were all nothin' but a bunch of glorified maids, cleanin' shit, moppin' floors, and cleanin' toilets. That's all they ever let us do. I decided to work the midnight to eight shift. I would get home about 8:20 in the morning in time to fix Randy's lunch, in time to get Cor and Randy off to school. Jennings was usually fairly independent. A lot of the neighbors thought I was leaving my children home on general principle, but you can't please the world. All I wanted to do was feed my kids, and put shoes on their feet, not shoes they wanted but shoes that they needed.

Cor was getting rapidly worse. My health was going to hell. My blood pressure had gone sky high. I was a walkin' time bomb. I was having cold sweats and the arthritis in my arm was hurting me so bad. I had really run myself ragged because I was averaging three hours of sleep a day, which was not a continual three hours either. Cor and Randy came home for lunch. Cor had to come home so that she could get her medication. A lot of my well-meaning friends used to ask me why I wouldn't let my kids eat free lunch at school since they were eligible for it. They didn't like the free lunch; it was the same free lunch that I ate twenty years ago. The stigma attached to free lunch is the same stigma that they had when I was a child. Now, the paying student eats the same lunch that the free kids eat. But a loud-mouthed teacher always gets at the head of the cafeteria and says, "Free lunch." They separate the kids and it makes them feel degraded and that they are saying, "Well, my parents are too poor to pay for my lunch. I'm a free luncheon."

I also needed to be home so that Cor could see me there. I could also give her the medication. So I allowed my children to come home at lunchtime. I'm always trying my best not to subject them to any emotional stresses and strains that I myself wouldn't like. I have always tried to project myself into their minds and its a very difficult transition to make. This is the way I try to deal with my kids. I'm not saying it's the right way and I'm not saying it's the wrong way. When raisin' my kids, I'm playin' it by ear.

I worked weekends and holidays, not out of choice. When you get hired last, you take all the shit days. I think I was off Tuesdays and Wednesdays, and when you work at Creedmore, you work. We had fifty-six patients on that ward in 1969 and 1970. I worked with an old lady who was about sixty-two. She worked two jobs to live. She had had a stroke and was partially paralyzed. From four-thirty in the morning to eight, we worked like dogs. We had to potty, dress, and feed fifty-six patients and make up their beds. We were overworked and underpaid. I felt so frustrated because there were so many needs that were left undone. But I loved the patients I worked with. I worked with nothin' but old ladies. They been here a long time and they can really tell you something. They're just a whole reservoir of knowledge.

I was also taking a creative writing course at this time. I was going to CCNY one night a week. I would leave class at nine forty-five and come from Harlem all the way to Creedmore to work the twelve to eight shift, so no wonder my blood pressure went up. My doctor had me up to 400 mg. a day of Equanil, of which I only took 100 mg., and he had me on special pills for arthritis in my arms. And, of course, I continued to work.

Dorothy, my neighbor downstairs, told me Cor wasn't sleeping and that I had to come home. I told her that I had to feed my kids. She told me what I looked like. I had lost 45 pounds. Dorothy said Cor was calling her on the telephone and saying she had a stomachache. She said Cor used to walk the floors until three or four in the morning. Cor couldn't sleep 'cause her fears were so real and big. But I didn't want to accept the fact that my child was going insane.

I would send Cor into the kitchen and tell her to fix her dinner plate while I fed the little ones. She'd go into the kitchen and take a hot cover off a pot, and rather than take the spoon and fork to take the spaghetti out of the pot, she took her bare hands and dug into the pot. She didn't feel the pain from the burning. I had to come and take it away from her and tell her to sit down. She became more compulsive in her eating habits. She wouldn't take a breath between mouthfuls. Cor had always wanted her parents together.

JOHN decided to sue me for adultery. I just thought he could have been kinder since I was his children's mother. I went to see my friend Bernard Lampen. I had petitioned for him when he was running for civil court judge in the Queens Village District. We would go from door to door, me with my big belly, to get the black vote. A lot of blacks will not vote, probably out of apathy which comes about from living conditions. They figure why the hell should they vote for a particular person, a guy like Nixon, who ain't interested in poor folks. You know, black people in particular and poor folks in general. I thought Bernie was a great guy and if anybody should have been in civil court it was Bernie. So I tried to get the black vote for him.

So I went to Bernie and I was scared to death. He thought it was hysterical that my husband was suing me for adultery. But Coretta, with the realization that divorce was coming, began to deteriorate rapidly. I tried to pretend it wasn't happening. She was with a new doctor, Dr. Duskow, and she was to be kept on Thorazine and Kemadrin which wards off the side effects of Thorazine like a very heavy hangover feeling, a stiff neck, and achiness in the head. I was immediately hostile to Dr. Duskow because I thought he was very indifferent. Coretta wanted to talk to him and he didn't allow her to. Her visits were fifteen minutes every Saturday and it appeared to me that they were just for Cor to pick up medication. I asked my friend June to take Coretta to Dr. Duskow just to make sure I wasn't being a racist in reverse. When she came back with Cor, Cor was very withdrawn and didn't want anybody to touch her. June said, "Take these goddamned pills and put 'em in the goddamned garbage. He's an indifferent, impersonal bastard."

I asked for a change of doctors in November. I was turned down. The clerk told me I could not get another doctor. This is how far you can go in a city hospital. I asked again in December and was turned down. In January I was turned down again. All Coretta was really doing was getting medication. It was hard for me to agree to putting Cor on medication in the first place, knowing what medication does to blood cells and to patients at Creedmore State Hospital. Cor was trying to talk to her doctor but he didn't want to hear a damn thing. All he wanted to do was get the chart out of the way. That's what Coretta was and all the other children who came to see him.

Cor never slept although she functioned very

well in school. She went from a fifth-grade level math to a sixth-plus level math in a period of six months. I couldn't accept that she wasn't sleeping, but she wasn't. On my pass night from Creedmore, Coretta, Randy, and I shared the same bedroom. Randy would sleep with me and Coretta had her own bed. She would lay awake nights, and in the middle of the night, scream and wake me up and say, "Mommy, Mommy, Mommy, did you lock the door?" Her paranoia and her fears were like monsters in the dark. She was afraid she was going to die. She was afraid to sleep with the lights out. Since my mother died, I was afraid of sleeping in the dark also. I was twenty-four years old before I stopped sleeping with the light on. I used to tell people I kept the light on in the bathroom so the kids wouldn't fall going to the bathroom. Well, that might have been a small reason, but the real reason was that I was afraid of sleeping in the dark. So Cor picked up that fear from me, only hers got all out of proportion.

Cor began to bicker with her brothers and sisters. I'd come home from work at eight thirty in the morning and Randy would be covered with scratches. Jennings and Randy didn't tell me what was going on because they didn't want to worry me. It was not until ten months after Cor had been hospitalized that my older son broke down hysterically. Ten months. He said, "Mommy, I knew she was going crazy, but I didn't want to worry you because I knew you had to work."

In the meantime, I was being served with that summons and subpeona to go to John's lawyer's office. Cor's illness was becoming more vivid and she was pulling me right into it with her. I knew she was miserable, but I couldn't help her. There was nothing I could do. I tried to reassure her of my love and that everything was going to be all right. At the meeting with John's attorney and my lawyer I had worked up to a fever pitch. All I could think of was losing the kids. I was really getting ready to flip out.

At the meeting with the attorneys, they asked us to step outside so that they could confer privately. I told John that I didn't want his alimony, I wanted to be independent. The kids, the prizes that he got for kids, should get the money. But I really wanted to talk to him about Cor. I begged him to visit her and tell her that everything was going to be all right regardless of the fact that we were getting a divorce. I pleaded with him to come and hold Cor in his arms and tell her that he loved her. Otherwise I knew that we would lose her. But I didn't think my child was going psychotic. I thought we were going to lose her to drugs or that she would start runnin' away from home and I'd be lookin' for her in Harlem or East New York or the Village. I thought she'd become one of the thousands of teenagers that run away away from home. John promised to come and see Coretta, but the next time he was to see her was in the adult female psychiatric ward at Elmhurst City Hospital, lying on a mattress in an isolated room completely sedated and out of it.

10

CORETTA had an appointment with Dr. Duskow April 10, 1970. It was the last appointment she was to have with him. I had cancelled a Saturday appointment to get her an appointment on a Friday so that he could see her longer. I told him that she desperately needed someone to talk to. I explained that she hadn't been on medication for at least a week because I had run out of pills. I left Coretta in there with him and told him to listen to her, not just talk at her. He had to see her more than once a month and not just for medication.

After ten minutes, Cor came out and handed me a prescription. He had increased the dosage of her medication. I met Dr. Duskow coming from his office down the hall. I told him that the new prescription would hit her system like LSD. He told me that he was the doctor and that I shouldn't question his integrity. Cor's next appointment was next month. I was so mad I wanted to scratch his eyeballs right out. All I could think about was Cor's misery.

Everytime I took Cor for an appointment, we had a day out. I took her for lunch or we'd go wish shoppin'. Wish shoppin' is when you do down Jamaica Avenue, or any old shoppin' district, and you look in the windows and you wish shop. We used to wish shop a lot. But when we went to lunch, I watched how she ate compulsively and stuffed her mouth and how she was shaking. She would say, "Mommy, if you give me those pills I'm gonna die. You're trying to poison me." And I had to explain how the doctor had watered them down and the doctor knew what was best for her, lying to myself.

Cor stayed up all night that night. I administered the second dosage around one o'clock that morning. She'd doze off for a while and then she'd jump up, and repeat those same questions again. "Mommy, am I gonna die if I go to sleep? Mommy, do you think the pills are going to poison me? Mommy, did you check the gas? Mommy, is the door locked? Mommy, are the windows locked?" And I would catnap in between and I would have her in bed with me and I'd sleep with my arms around her. I'd doze off and go off into a deep sleep and I'd wake up about fifteen minutes later and realize she was out of the bed. I'd come out into the living room and she'd have the television on or she'd be in the kitchen and she'd be boiling water for some reason. She didn't know what she wanted.

Sunday I had to go to a meeting at Cardoza High School. Classes were being boycotted for dealing with white history only, not black and white history. When I came home that night, all the children in the house were asleep except for Cor. She had taken all the clothes out of the closet and was crawling around on the floor and tying them up in little bundles. The house was a wreck. I didn't ask her why she was tying up little bundles of clothes.

Everything was bizarre to her. I gave her another dosage and urged her to come to bed. All night long until daybreak, she was picking things off the floor that weren't there. My biggest fear was that if I went to sleep, I would wake up and find that all of us had been murdered. She would put out all the lights and pick, pick, pick things that weren't there, off the floor, off the walls. I don't know what she was seeing, but whatever it was, it was physical and real to her. I dozed off about five with Cor next to me and woke up about fifteen minutes later and Cor wasn't there. I jumped up and checked the other children and they were all right. Cor was in the kitchen at the stove watchin' a pot, and it had turned almost white hot. I took her by the hand and I said, "Come on Cor, Mommy wants you to lie down." I was so exhausted and my baby hadn't been asleep for almost three days.

I woke Jennings and Randy and told them to get dressed for school because I didn't want them to see their sister go. I was combin' Cor's hair, and she said, "Mommy, you see that. Jennings just hit me." And Jennings was still in the bedroom, sittin' on the edge of the bed, because he hadn't even gotten up good. I told her that Jennings couldn't have hit her but she didn't hear me. She kept insisting that Jennings hit her.

My phone rang and it was one of my friends that worked at Creedmore with me. Claude hadn't seen me for a couple of days so he called me to ask me why I hadn't been to work. So he says, "Hiya Penny, how ya doin'?" I said "Claude, my child is going," and he says, "What you mean your child's goin'?" And I said, "My child, the one who's disturbed." I used to talk to him on the bus. We had become close friends even though he had never been to my house. We had things in common because I was going to school one night a week and trying to matriculate and he was going to law school. And he said, "I know you could tell me it's none of my business, but you need somebody." Claude had never been to my house. Claude was here in ten minutes. I don't know where he came from. Then I called June and I said, "June, you got to take me to the hospital. You can't go into work today." "Okay, honey," June said, "I'll be right there." June was always on the spot. So I sent Jennings and Randy to school, and I noticed how Jennings clung to Randy and Randy clung to Jennings 'cause they knew something was wrong. I didn't know that Jennings had known that Cor had gone psychotic.

The baby started to cry and Coretta said, "Mommy, should I go pick up the baby?" And I said, "No, Coretta." She went to walk down the hall and then she said, "No, I better not pick him up. I might drop him." That's the last thing that Cor said to me that made any sense. The rest of it was bizarre, broken, and I still couldn't believe that she was going. I got her clothes ready and told her to get dressed. She went down the hall and came back out of the room and she was trying to put on a blouse that belonged to Randy on her legs. Now I knew she was gone. I had to dress my child like I had to dress my patients out at Creedmore. We got in June's car and she didn't even know she was in a car. Cor just talked outa her mind and every once in a while reality would come back and she would say, "June, Mommy, June, Mommy."

We got to Queens Hospital Center. I walked up the stairs to the clinic and June was behind me with Lamumba in her arms. I went into the waiting room and I said, "I want to see Dr. Duskow right now. And before they could ring up Dr. Duskow, I was in his office because I wasn't waitin' to be announced. I figured I had paid my dues. I had a pocket full of the pills that he had prescribed for my daughter, and I took the pills and I slammed them down on the desk, and I said, "My child is psychotic. She has to be hospitalized. Now what you gonna do about that, Dr. Duskow?"

The first thing he did (he was on the defensive immediately), sitting in his chair and holding tight to his seat, was tell me that he could change the medication. I said, "A bomb wouldn't bring her down. I want a bed for my daughter now." He said, "We don't have any beds. Take her to Creedmore." "Take her to where?" I said, and he said, "To Creedmore." And I said, "Before I take her to Creedmore State Hospital, that snake pit, I'll cut her throat from ear to ear and let her bleed to death on your desk." Then he said, "This woman's hysterical," and I got ready to punch him.

Another doctor just happened to be passin' by the office and he heard all this hell I was raisin' 'cause Dr. Duskow was ten motherfuckers. I didn't bite my tongue. I used street language on that son of a bitch because that's what he deserved and he understood it. He understood every word because I had been there three days earlier beggin' him to see my child more often and listen to her. And he never did get out of his seat to go in the waitin' room to see Cor. This other doctor said I wasn't hysterical and that Cor was definitely psychotic. "She's going to have to be hospitalized, Dr. Duskow," he said, "and the worst thing about it is we don't have a damn bed for her. If more mothers would come up to hospitals and raise the hell that she raised, perhaps we would be equipped to take care of patients such as these." I told Dr. Duskow I was taking Cor to Elmhurst City Hospital.

So June, Lamumba, Claude, Cor, and I made our way to Elmhurst City Hospital. Cor and I immediately crossed Parsons Boulevard to get to the car and everybody followed us. We got in the middle of traffic and Cor turned around and attacked me. She started punchin' me brutally in the face and kickin' me and I have helped subdue many, many psychotic patients, but I could not bring up the strength to subdue my child. I screamed to Claude that the traffic was comin' and I had to let her keep beating me because I didn't want her to run away and get hit by a car. Claude took her and got in the back of the car with her. I was in the front with June and the baby. That Lamumba is a soldier, honey. He knew what was going on. But he was so pleasant. I didn't even stop to feed him breakfast. I just had him a bottle of orange juice.

When we got into the emergency clinic at Elmhurst City Hospital, the fact that Cor was born in that hospital just hit me. Cor was still out of her head. The whole emergency clinic was filled up.

You always find this in a city hospital. I believe people have died waiting to see a damned doctor. They told me I was number fifty somethin'. I told them my child had to go to the mental hygiene clinic, and they very nicely told me to sit down and wait. So I told Claude, "Don't hold her. Let her go." And we let Cor go and she walked up to a woman and was about ready to snatch the woman's baby. She got ready to climb over the counter that protects the clerks from the sick patients. You better believe that they gave me her chart and told me to go directly to the hygiene clinic. We got out of there and we walked to the clinic and there was another line. I'm not saying that I should be first because I was tired of waitin' for 400 years. But I am saying that when a patient is suffering from any kind of illness that is immediately detrimental to himself, or to someone else, then *move*. But they got to wait until they see pourin' blood and somebody droppin' dead before they jump and do something. Claude asked me if he should hold Cor and I told him to let her go. Cor ran out of the mental hygiene clinic into a doctor's office, snatched his eyeglasses off his eyes and knocked everything he had on his desk off. You better believe they saw me.

The doctor asked me how long Cor had been under treatment. I explained the whole story to him. He said that my child was like a child who had been on a bummer LSD trip. He asked if my child had been out of the house and I told him that Coretta had always been the only one of my children who stayed close to me and was always under my feet. Constantly. I did not associate with people who dropped acid. Would like to. I don't even smoke pot. Would like to. Don't snort cocaine, would like to. I would like to stay high as ten motherfuckers, but you can't deal with what's relevant high. So, he called upstairs and asked did they have a bed in children's psychiatric and they said no. Then he said, "Get one." It was like he was glad that finally there was a mother who came in there and helped him push for a bed. I wasn't gonna turn around because I knew there was no other place for Cor to go but to Creedmore.

After that it took me almost an hour to get her processed into the hospital. They were putting her in the female adult psychiatric ward and I got very nervous. She was just a child and anything could happen to her up there. Wards aren't that heavily staffed and I didn't want my child exposed to any sexual or physical abuses. I took her, by myself, up in the elevator to this ward. I heard the key open this big lock and the nurse took her, and I kissed her. She didn't even realize that I kissed her. When they closed that door I thought I was going to die. My heart stopped. I looked through that wire mesh window and it was worse than the feeling a mother has after the baby comes out and the cord is cut. You realize the baby is not completely dependent on you and I guess that's where the mothers' blues comes from. But I felt worse. The Cor who I loved so much was completely overwhelmed by the other Cor. And I peeped through that window and I wanted to cry and break down and scream, but I had to think about the other children. I had to be strong because I knew this was just the beginning of Cor's hell.

I went home and all my friends just came to me. Everybody was there that I knew. I called the Air Base and I talked to the officer on duty there and he told me that John was out of the country and they were having trouble with his plane, but as soon as they heard from him they would get in touch with me. The base I'm referring to is McGuire Air Force Base in Fort Dix, New Jersey. I tried to find out from them what kind of hospital insurance I could get for Cor. I had to go through a complete description of her psychotic breakdown. And it just wore me out.

Sometimes when I'm feeling at my lowest, when I'm taking advantage of feeling sorry for myself, when I've felt like maybe I'm being prepared for a crucifixion, I begin to think of things that have happened to other human beings. I bring myself back to a parable that my Grandmother Johnson used to tell us about a group of people who were sitting around complaining about how hard their individual lives were. They all decided to put their problems in a bag. They were going to blindfold themselves and walk to the center of the room and put their problem bags in the center of the floor. Then they were supposed to take their blindfolds off and search for the smallest bag. And my grandmother used to say that all the bags looked so big and full of problems that everyone in the room was trying to find their own bag with their own problems. So, even though my problems seem so monumental and insurmountable, I'd still rather keep my own bag. So, I'm not waving my flag and saying my problems are worse than yours. But I can only think that some unseen force or that unseen whatever that was left to protect us after my mother was murdered has helped me to cope with my problems. When I think of all my brothers and sisters have been through, I realize we could have turned out much worse. The only thing society says we have done wrong is getting pregnant.

Lyn Dobrin came to the house, which looked like a tornado hit it, to get Lamumba. She took a paper bag out of the closet, packed the little stuff that he had, and said "Goodbye, Penny." She did what any friend would do. And Lyn is one of my vanilla sisters. She's not a liberal. She's a white, she's a realist, and she's a very warm human being. The next day she brought groceries and four loaves of meat loaf that she baked and left. Lamumba is her and her husband Arthur's godchild. If anything happens to me or Lamumba's father, they would take and raise him and school him for me because they love him. But Lamumba is such a handful that Lyn always tells me, "Please don't die!" Between Ketori, her adopted child (some people call her an "inter-racial" baby but I don't know what "inter-racial" is) and Lamumba, she'd catch hell.

My other neighbors saw to Randy and Jennings because I was like a madwoman. My pressure was hittin' and missin' about 220, 200. My pulse was 120 a minute and it was supposed to only be 80. Lola, Warren, Leslie, and Ollie were there to help me. Lola took me to the hospital every day.

The first visit to come was twenty-four hours after I left Cor there. The nurse led us to a room called "Isolation." In a mental hospital, it's where you isolate patients who are abusive and violent and harmful to themselves and others. The room is always bare of furniture, except for a mattress on the floor. I immediately knew my baby was in the isolation room, because when the door was opened I saw the slot that they put food through. It's like a cage. And I never thought that I would see my Coretta there.

The nurse tried to pull Cor to her feet, but she was heavily sedated. It must have taken intramuscular injections and all kinds of things to keep Cor down, because she needed to rest, she had to have the rest, she hadn't been sleepin' for seventy-two hours. So I got down on my knees (the nurse thought I was breaking down, but I told her, "That's all right, I'm not breaking down. Everything's all right"), I put my face on Cor's face, and I put my mouth to her ear, and said, "Corry, it's Mommy; Mommy loves you, everything is gonna be all right." She said, "Mommy, my arms hurt so bad." When she told me that, I assumed that she had been in a straitjacket. Of course, they would not let me see her in a straitjacket, but I knew that she had been violent and abusive, and that they would have to subdue her somehow. So I knew whatever the attendants and the nurses had to do wasn't done out of meanness. The nurses and attendants at Elmhurst City Hospital were very good to my Cor. I know she was not abused in any way. I think they were very concerned because they knew how concerned I was.

We came out of the ward and immediately bumped into Major John, Cor's father, who said he wanted her so much. I didn't know what I was going to say to him, because the night before he had called me up from New Jersey, not even twelve hours after I put my child in the hospital, not even two weeks after I'd begged him to come and see her and hold her and reassure her that he loved her. The first thing that son of a bitch said to me was that he talked to the admitting doctor and the admitting doctor told him that Cor reacted like a child on LSD. He was standing there indicting me, trying to put guilt feelings on me, trying to insinuate that either I had given Cor LSD, or that I was keeping company with acid heads. That's about how much respect he has for me. I wanted to spit in his face. I calmly tried to tell him that Cor had to be in a private hospital. I could not put her in Creedmore. We had to work together to find a hospital for her. I knew it was no time to scratch his eyes out or spit in his face.

Two days later he told me that one of his colleagues told him that there were no hospitals. The only hospitals available for Cor's illness were state hospitals. I told him what he could do with his colleague and himself. I told him that if Rockefeller's twelve-year-old daughter had a psychotic breakdown, his daughter wouldn't go to a state hospital. That's why my daughter wasn't goin' to one. And I couldn't reach him; this man couldn't understand. I'm trying to tell him that my grandmother died in Pilgrim State Hospital because of indifference, inadequate personnel. My sister was in and out of mental hospitals all her life. And I worked in the same hell-hole he wanted me to put my child in. Well, he didn't grow up in my shoes. He didn't clean shit at Creedmore and he didn't see the shit I saw happening to the human beings at Creedmore.

I called my mother-in-law and I tried to console her. I described what had happened to Coretta and that through the years that she was disturbed I was taking her back and forth to doctors. She, too, would not accept the fact that Coretta was mentally and emotionally disturbed. Do you know what that bitch had the nerve to say to me? She said, "Penny, did you maybe give her an overdose of medication?" Like I was so inhuman or so stupid or so ignorant to give my baby an overdose of medication.

Eventually, after what I thought would be endless searching and frustration, we found High Point Hospital through this social worker at Elmhurst City Hospital. The government would pay all expenses. This hospital costs $1,750 a month. If you don't have insurance, or if you're not rich, you don't stand a chance of being in a controlled and protective environment. Everything costs money! Any ordinary person who has a breakdown would have to eventually end up in a state hospital.

High Point is a beautiful hospital that almost looks like a utopia. It's a big estate on lots of grounds. The doctor who runs the hospital bought the estate and started his own hospital. Coretta is the only black patient there. She's the first black patient and the youngest patient they've ever had. She told the doctor who signed her in that she didn't want to stay there because there were so many white people and they were gonna lynch her. But Coretta was tucked away in High Point Hospital and I was not to be allowed to see her for three to six weeks. They wanted to observe her and orient her to the hospital. I felt very bad as a mother, but I knew she was safe so I accepted it. It seemed like the battle was over for a while. I had to come home and try to get my other kids into a regulated routine.

11

I'D LIKE to tell about George Brown. I went to a party at my girl friend Gwynne's house. She was trying to hook me up with fellows, right? So she had two or three brothers in there, right? All you got to do to be a brother is get you an Afro wig and a dashiki, right? Twenty-five dollars and you're a brother.

I didn't want to go to the party but since it was so close I told Gwynne okay. So these brothers are in there. She was playing Dick Gregory's record "The Light Side and the Dark Side," which is great, you know, but nobody really wanted to listen to it. In fact, the first thing that happened was that these guys zeroed in on these buttons I was wearin'. I had on "Free the New York 21" and "Power to the People" and "War is Not Healthy for Little Children and Other Living Things." I had my buttons on. I bought 'em, they were mine. Well, immediately these brothers began to attack my buttons. "Why you wear that? I don't believe in 'Power to the People.'" "Well," I said, "I believe in all power to the correct people whoever they may be, whether they be black, white or grizzly gray." So. I was really very touchy about the Panthers because I felt very close to them. Especially the East Coast 21. My heart was just with 'em all the time.

Then the bell rang and in walks this little puny-lookin' dude. He had buck teeth and reddish wavy hair, bright blue eyes, and beautiful lines in his face. Well, when I say beautiful lines, I mean a man who has real rugged lines in his face, deep impressions in his face. You know that he's wise; you can see wisdom and depth in his face. He came in with a bottle and I found out that he didn't drink because he had ulcers, and his name was George Brown. Everybody got very close-mouthed because a honky walked into the party, right? But he was very civilized and I was busy tryin' to listen to the record and block these niggers out who was tellin' me that they didn't dig my Panther buttons. I wouldn't get involved with the dudes because how am I going to get emotionally involved with a dude who doesn't make sense or relate to my political beliefs or things that I see and live and know? So, I cut these dudes right off, 'cause I didn't want to hear nothing they had to say. Everybody had drinks and I'm trying to listen to the record, and they kept harassin' me; they wanted to know about those buttons. We all ended up around the table with Dick Gregory in the background, soft, and I noticed that George was sittin' at the table, very, very quiet. And I was peepin' at him, 'cause I was lookin' at the lines in his face and just watchin' how normal he was actin'. You know, he wasn't uptight about being in a house with nothin' but blacks at an informal party. The brothers began to discuss the Panther buttons again, and one of them asked George, "Hey, man, where you come from?" He said, "My parents are English and French and we're the bastards who started it all. And I overheard the remarks toward the lady's buttons here, but I've been out of this country for quite a few years now." George is a seaman, he's a captain. He's had a ship in Martinique and the West Indies, and he goes from island to island. That's how he made his money. His whole family has a history of whalers and seamen. They all come from Bedford, Massachusetts.

"But from what I've seen," he continued, "since I've been back, if I was a black man, I couldn't be nothing but a Panther. Otherwise I couldn't face myself as a man." And then he went on to say that he was raised to love everything that was warm and alive, even animals and human beings, and that he was never taught racism. In the town he came from, he never saw a black person until he was eighteen years old in the Navy. He said, "From what my mother taught me when she was alive and raisin' me, I could never be inhuman to another human being. From what I've seen since I've been back, the shit is gonna hit the fan, and I will be one of the many blue eyes that will be up on a roof with a high-powered rifle shootin' other blue eyes."

Well, goddamn! When this dude came out with this garbage, after these brothers had just attacked me about my buttons, I said to myself, "Hmmm, that's all right. Now the party's interesting." Here Gwynne was trying to fix me up with these brothers, and politically we weren't reaching each other. That's why everything that appears to be black ain't necessarily so. Blackness is a state of mind. And the racism can be just as bad comin' from blacks as whites. What I think most of us are looking for, us deranged people out here . . . you hear all this about human rights . . . human dignity . . . is a human family. This is why I hate to put color on people because from that point on I felt very close to George because he was honest. No, he wasn't honest, he was a realist. And he left them so-called brothers sittin' there with their mouths hanging out. They asked him one question and he went on to tell them that he was French and English, and was one of the sons of bitches that started it all. Well, this was a revelation to me. This was a man talkin'.

So, we wound up sitting on top of the record player listenin' to "The Light Side and the Dark Side" and we really had a good time. I just forgot all about the rest of the niggers and I said to myself, this old whitey can't be true.

Gwynne had a flat tire, and nobody offered to help her but George. So I said, "Gwynne, I'll go with you." George thought he could fix it and he's a little guy. He only weighs 130 pounds but he takes a size 13 shoe. George was the manager at Cunningham. But he had chosen to live in the black belt. He was livin' back there with the niggers in Cunningham Heights. We went into his apartment because he had to get a key for the jack to his tire. And I said to myself, "Watch this honky get Roman hands and Russian fingers." Nine times out of ten, the average white dude walking the streets today figures that a sister is more sensuous than a white sister. We were all taught the same puritanical bullshit, all of us. Quite naturally, the first thing a white man will do to you, especially your boss, or the foreman on the job, is pat you on the ass, or somethin'. They don't have no respect for you because you ain't nothin' but a wench. Between bein' a wench, a slave, and a female, you don't get much respect. But George was such a gentleman. We went to the garage, got the jack and started talkin' about O'Hara's writing and my kids. He liked Ernest Hemingway and we talked about Ernest Hemingway.

When we got back to Gwynne's house, the party was still goin' on, but I didn't see nobody 'cause I didn't want to hear nothin' those other folks had to say. I can't go to a party, I can't go to a bar and not talk about what's relevant. What's relevant is oppression and man's inhumanity to man. I can't sit and talk about the latest show because I'm too poor to go to the movies. If I did have the money, I wouldn't waste my time. The only way I can socialize is to get into a discussion.

I had to check on my kids because I didn't have a sitter and George asked me if he could go along. He came into my junky old house and saw my cinderblock-and-boards library. He thought that was an out-of-sight way to build a library. He said, "Penny, you've got so many books here." We went back to Gwynne's, and he said to me, "Penny, would you come to my house with me and read my manuscript?" And I read some of his writing, and if I ever see George Brown again (he's in the West Indies now), I hope that I can convince him to finish his novel, because what I read had so much feeling in it that I sat there with tears in my eyes. I said, "I didn't know honkies had feelings."

He ended up comin' over to my house and reading part of the manuscript that I had been working on and didn't leave until six o'clock in the morning.

After that, we started to go out together. Every evening George would come from the racetrack, and we would walk together, and talk, talk. He was so nice. In fact, he was so comfortable that I went to his house one night to help him figure out the horses and he already had glasses in the freezer compartment frosted for beer. And I used to have my beer. This one night I had gas, and I was plannin' on a little lovin', you know, trying to get rid of my hangups, white and black, black and white. The first thing I do when I see a white man, if he wants to get interested in me, is project my thoughts back to the past when we were being bought and sold. I would feel very resentful when I thought about that buying and selling us into slavery, the master buying us, because I would say to myself, "We're priceless people. How could anyone put a price on us?" So when I would see a white man, this would be my hangup. I never used to talk to white men because I thought they had that attitude, that preconceived idea of somebody who's been the master, right? On top of that, I've never been too trusting of men anyway, so when I meet a white man, it's twice as bad. Besides, I figure, "Give the brothers a chance. I'm a strong and understanding black woman who loves the black exslave male in this country. For thirty years I've been trying to preserve myself for a black brother who would deserve me, who should have a strong black sister, being as we're just starting to meet each other." But if that George Brown ever comes around again, the black brothers is gonna blow me.

So this night I'm getting rid of my hangups, right? And I had hypnotized myself into thinking, "Okay, when you see George Brown you ain't gonna see color." I really got myself all psyched up, because I was gonna get this little dude with the size 13 shoe, this little bitty man. But I had gas and I had to break wind. So I had to say, "George, I got gas." I can barely walk when I got gas. It locks in my intestines. And I can't break wind, can't pass it, and it hurts like hell. So George made me get on my hands and knees in a jackknife position, and then he said, "Penny, what else helps it?" I said, "Hot water, right from the faucet, with lemon juice in it." It's the only thing that will cut the gas for me. And then I can break wind with the best of them.

Well, see, I had counted on givin' a little bit. I was gonna give George Brown some . . . you know what . . . yes, I was, and there instead I was in a jackknife position and he was bringin' me lemon juice and hot water and I was fartin'. And that was the extent of our romantic escapade.

George Brown came and stayed with us in Westbury at Arthur and Lyn Dobrin's house. They offered me their house for the summer while they went to organize the Ethical Humanist Camp in Arizona. George and I were both afraid of our own emotions. We're very emotional people. He said he loved the way I cared about my children. He said it was so beautiful because when I used to talk about my kids, my face used to shine. And when you talked to George he would look you in the face. He would never be looking this way or that way. You knew damn well he was listening.

He said we should get together and go to Martinique. His biggest dream was to get his own boat so he could take me and the kids around the world. But he always told me, well, we can't leave Cor. He never saw my daughter, but from the trips I made up there on Sunday, and the way he heard me talk about her, he felt like he knew her. He told my friend June that he was supposed to have left for the West Indian Islands two weeks before Randy's birthday. He said the only thing that was keeping him here was me. June was shocked because she didn't know how he felt. He told her that I needed somebody to take care of me because I was so alone. He was the first male I ever met that ever picked it up that I was alone. I mean really alone. Because you have a lot of friends coming to your house and you know a lot of people, when you face your real problems and you have to make a decision, and you close the door on your two-by-four apartment, you're all alone if you don't have anybody close to you.

He was gonna give Randy a big party and buy her what she wanted. She wanted a guitar and he wanted to buy Lamumba a rockin' horse. He was makin' all kinds of plans. But he never showed up to the party. I don't know what happened, but the only thing that I could tell June was that there's a possibility he went home and had second thoughts. I guess he realized that if he were to commit himself to me and the children, he would have to never, never want to short-change me. So rather than just stay for a while and take from me, he just left. But knowin' George was good for me and I can only wish him happiness.

12

CORETTA was the only child I had that could not draw things as they really were. Randy, when she draws herself, draws herself tall and strong and black with a real short natural. She draws the way she looks with a big smile and red lips and big white teeth smiling, and she draws me with bushy hair and big earrings and bright colors and a beautiful smile. And she draws the brother, the black male, with the woolly head and the sideburns and the beard, very healthy and strong, a whole figure. Jennings draws people in detail the way he sees them. He likes to draw most of his drawings about wars because at the age he's at, he's surrounded by wars or ruins of wars. He draws Chinese people Chinese. He draws black people black. He draws white people white. You know what he's drawing. Coretta is the only child that I've ever had that was never able to draw the male figure whole. I mean the top part of the body. She's always drawn me white with the bouffant blonde hair and the blue eyes and the fake lashes and she's always drawn herself white, the family white, everything white.

During those months in late 1969 and early 1970 that Cor was breaking down, Randy didn't have much of me 'cause I was so absorbed in Cor's sickness that I just didn't hold her like I used to. I guess I was feeling like such a failure. I was feeling so guilty and sorry for myself. One day I told Mrs. Charles, my counselor, that I couldn't hold Randy like I used to and that I was sort of rejecting her. Mrs. Charles asked me what kind of little girl was Randy. And I told her how smart she was and how she liked school and how she had built a bumper against all the big things that had happened to her. She functions so well in school that the principal of the school that my kids have gone to for the last six years did not know that I had a third child in school. Then Mrs. Charles asked me what kind of little girl I was. I began to tell her and automatically realized that Randy's a lot like me, the way I used to be when I was a little girl. Consequently, I was rejecting Randy because I was feeling like shit. (Mrs. Charles is now Assistant Dean for Student Development at York College. She is a student counselor. Dean Marsh [Venis], my friend and comrade, had asked her to counsel me as a favor to him.)

I JUST wanted to curl up into a cocoon, but you can't. You have to keep facing reality. Lyn and Arthur's house in Westbury seemed to fall apart as soon as I got there. Hannibal, our dog, was with us. We named him after the African warrior who crossed the Alps and lived in southern Italy for 250 years. We all thought Hannibal looked like Victor Mature, right on. And we thought Cleopatra was Elizabeth Taylor, right on. We learned differently. Anyway, Hannibal was chewing everything up in sight they had there in their house. He had gotten an allergy and had gotten sick and I had to spend money for shots for him.

Jennings was acting out. He was frustrated. Jennings had always been a very progressive, intelligent, and aggressive black male child. But at P.S. 135, the people couldn't relate to him. He was always catching hell because he has always been a very aware child, a very perceptive child. I had to take Jennings out of P.S. 135 in Queens three weeks before school was over. When he heard Nixon speak in 1969 on the escalation of the Vietnam War and why we were not going to leave Vietnam, he wrote an answer:

> *Vietnam, Vietnam, as bloody as a woman's first child*
> *More fire than a napalm's hell, more laughter than a dead man's stone*
> *Vietnam, Vietnam, what have you done to my black son?*

He was relating to the black troops that were there. We all know that the biggest percentages of the deaths in Vietnam are blacks. A lot of sisters, white and black, are saying that that's genocide. This is what they had to deal with at P.S. 135.

One day I had put Lamumba in my arms, he was only about four weeks old, and I walked down to that school in answer to a letter that Mrs. King, Jennings' teacher, had sent me saying that he wasn't doing his work, "please sign here." Jennings does not have a mother that signs anything there. I brought Lamumba in my arms with my diaper bag to let her know that she was disturbing me. When I got to class, I peeked in the back and I noticed that all the black students were in the back of the class. I don't know whether it's unconscious racism or not. I do not know, but I've seen this in many, many classes. I asked Mrs. King if I could speak to her. I like to make impromptu visits to teachers. I don't like them to prepare to see me because I like to see them in all their glory. I'm not doubting teachers, because my children, especially Randy, have had some very humanistic teachers. These teachers have not smashed her desire to learn. She's been fortunate because she's had teachers who want to teach. God only knows how they do with thrity-five to forty students a day.

I told Mrs. King that I noted she had Jennings in the back of the room and that Jennings had an eye defect and had she seen it on his health records? She said this was not on his health record. I told her perhaps she was having a problem with Jennings because she hadn't bothered to find out that an opthalmologist was preparing to make up a prescription for his eyes. He does have a lazy eye. I also told her that if she had bothered, she would have found out that Jennings lived with a disturbed sister.

She told me that Jennings asked too many questions. I told her that I allowed him to question me. Therefore, I felt he had a right to question her and that if I were a teacher, I wouldn't think I was teaching too well if my students didn't question me. Jennings asked relevant questions that those teachers couldn't deal with. I couldn't deal with all the questions he's asked me. But I wasn't goin' to hand down the continuous vicious cycle of the black mother beating the black male in order to keep the black male from being sold into slavery or being killed by the authority, meaning Master, or the police, or some racist dog.

The only thing that this teacher was interested in was the fact that she would have to move her whole class to put Jennings in front. So I told her I didn't care what she did but I wanted Jennings in front. She said if she moved him he would think he was special. And I told her he was, since he had an eye defect and besides, if I had a problem child in the class, I would put him in front. Mrs. Sands, the principal, suggested that Jennings be put in one of the two classes taught by black teachers because maybe he would relate better to a black teacher. And I told Mrs. Sands that she knew better than that. She knew that Jennings related to human beings on a one-to-one basis and that him having a black teacher wasn't gonna better the conditions, especially if the teacher had a white mind.

I asked them not to put Jennings in a black teacher's class, especially in a black female's class, because I did not want his spirit to be broken. But they moved Jennings to a black teacher's class anyway, a Mrs. Clauson. Later on I got a letter from school stating that Mrs. Clauson was going to expel Jennings. I went into school and asked why he was threatened with expulsion and I was told that Jennings used a lot of physical force on other children. Sure he uses physical force. When we first moved to Queens Village, Jennings used to get stoned. White kids used to ring around my son and throw rocks on his little bald head. He used to come home and tell me that while he was playing basketball a basketball hit his head. He used to have gashes in his skull and he never told me that these white kids would sit him in the middle of a circle and chant, "nigger, nigger, nigger." It took a white kid downstairs to come upstairs to tell me. He told me he was going to have to teach Jennings how to fight because he was out there lettin' them kids whip his ass.

Jennings was struck with a hockey stick on his head by a sixteen-year-old white kid in Cunningham Heights and I told that child that he did not have to do that to Jennings and that they should not play hockey where the young children are. He told me he'd do it again and raised the stick and I punched him in the jaw and I told him that white people weren't letting us live in Cunningham Heights. We paid our rent just like anybody else. I knew that they thought that we came from nothing but Jennings' father was in Vietnam fighting to protect that kid's pink balls and that if he put his hands on my son again, I'd kill him.

So I promised Jennings I wasn't going to send him back to P.S. 135, even if I had to teach him at home. I was just gonna boycott that school. I couldn't send Jennings there and let him go through the humiliation. And I couldn't let the teachers go through what Jennings was going to sock to 'em 'cause they can't deal with it. Jennings had developed a very hostile feeling toward being attacked by anyone. One day, Jennings' friend Tommy found a dime in the street and said it was

his. A group of kids said it was theirs and they
wanted to beat his behind. Jennings tried to tell
them that Tommy was his friend, and even if
Tommy wasn't his friend, they couldn't just jump
on him because he found a dime. Tommy was just
a kid and Jennings told them not to jump on him.
Consequently, Jennings almost got his throat cut
up. You know, he didn't tell me that one of them
kids put a knife to his throat. He didn't tell me.
What a pussy.

And P.S. 135 was so glad to get rid of him that
they didn't even send a truant officer to my house.
That's how glad they were of getting rid of Jennings. And this was the beginning of his trippin'
out and flippin' out. I was trying to deal with Jennings and love him and understand him. And this
is when he began to go to the Learning Tree
School, an experimental school, a free school. Most
of the children who came to the school were white,
middle-class boys between the ages of four-and-a-
half and fourteen. Most of the children had some
problems in public school. They couldn't cope with
the competition, the pressure, the regimentation. At
the free school they could learn about anything
they wanted to and could mingle with different age
children and learn how to make human relationships work.

I felt worried at first because Jennings wasn't going to be around many black students. Well, black
is a state of mind. The first day I put him in school
the older students were not there because they had
gone to see a picture that some blacks had put
together in Algiers. It was about the beginning of

the Black Panther Party. I had already taken Jennings to see it earlier. So I said, Jesus Christ, any kind of school that's relevant enough to take kids to see something that is relevant, that they want to see, gosh it's out of sight. In fact, the free-school older kids wanted to go to the 21 trial and they went.

Jennings acted out at the free school. He started throwing chairs around. Jennings had a lot of hang-ups about his father and his sister. He had a lot of guilt feelings that he couldn't deal with. But at the free school they all helped him by understanding him and loving him and caring about him. And my dear friend Clary, who I met there, is one of the parent-teachers who really helped. Jennings is studying biology and ninth-grade math while at P.S. 135 he was only studying sixth-grade math. When Jennings was in public school he used to fake homework rather than do it. He used to spend more time outside the principal's office than he did in class.

In the free school nobody was shocked because he wanted to learn about the female's menstrual cycle. I mean when his sister first got her menstrual cycle, he was so excited that his sister was makin' eggs that he would interject this into his Health Class where they were studying which came first, the chicken or the egg, right? So Jennings got up and asked the teacher a very relevant question; he asked her if a woman could get impregnated during her menstrual cycle. Now, the only thing he got from the teacher was, "Wow, I don't know." So Jennings came home and asked me for some obstetrics-gynecology books. He wanted to take the books to his teacher so she could find the answer. The woman already had two children and had probably gone through menopause.

Jennings still wants to be an architect and an oceanographer because he believes that the cities are going to be built underwater when he's a man. And he wants to be a surgeon too. Whatever Jennings wants to be, I know he will be. And keeping him in an experimental school is not going to keep him from being whatever he wants to be because he knows it's his life. And as long as my children do something to better conditions for their people and humanity in general, then I done my duty.

Jennings is on his way now. We started talking late one night and he finally told me how he felt about Cor's breakdown. And he said, "Mommy, I knew she was going crazy. But I didn't want to tell you. I didn't want to worry you. How come I think I'm stronger than you are, Mommy, when I come from you?" I told him that was the way life was and it was good that he thought he was stronger than me because perhaps at times he was. That's the mornin' he broke down and went hysterical about how his sister didn't love him and how he knew she loved him. And I told him, just like Clary told him, that Cor's sickness is what caused her to relate like she did. And perhaps he was the only male figure she could pile all her hostility on. And he was strong enough to hold on—the fucko that he was—he's gonna be all right.

13

You may have been wondering what has happened to René during all this. I had subjected myself to an exile from René because he couldn't be what I wanted him to be. They say you can't teach an old dog new tricks. He asked me to give up my other children to John since John was young, a professional, and capable of taking care of the kids financially. The love I had for René began to trickle away after he said this when I was six months' pregnant. He knew how I felt about my children because when he met me I made sure he met my children at the same time so he could understand what he was dealing with.

I remember when John found out that I was pregnant. I was terrified that he would take my children away from me. I was so upset that I called up René who was in Boston and asked him to come to the house. He knew those children are my heartbeat. So he got to my apartment and said, "Come on baby. I'm gonna take you out and I'm gonna buy you some filet mignon." So I put my hands back on my hips with my six months' belly looking like I was ten months and I said, "I don't want no fish!" And he said, "Penny, filet mignon ain't fish. Filet mignon is steak." He took me out to this restaurant and he ordered. Because it was so small I ate three. It wasn't until René asked me if I was ready for dessert that I happened to look up on the menu and saw what that filet mignon cost. But it was good. You know what hit me then, you know what hit me at that point was here I had lived twenty-eight years, a life of surviving, and I didn't know that filet mignon is steak. I thought it was fish, honey!

I had to separate myself from René for nine months before I could actually see him or talk to him to get him out of my system but I finally did it. When I see him he's an old man who could have been made young by involving himself with me and my children. I can only wish him love and happiness if he has time for it. I know that I have his child and this child is my total responsibility. Lamumba is mine. I made the decision to bring him into the world and not abort him. I loved his father and I love Lamumba. But I don't love his father anymore.

I don't want to slander him. I don't want to hurt him either. But I'm so fuckin' tired of this motherfucker, this dead nigger. By the way, I use the word "nigger" because "nigger" is used in the black kindgom no matter how European we become or African we stay. We use the term "nigger" very frequently and we use different intonations. Like Clary's white, but when she brings her kids to my house and they bad and they don't act right, I tell 'em, "Get outside you niggers. Stop making so much noise." I use the term frequently around my house due to the fact if the term is used toward my sons or my daughters, they won't feel so offended when the racists use it loosely. I feel if

I use it very loosely in my house, it will not cause any of my children to end up in prison or get killed on a bummer because somebody called you nigger. "Nigger" is anything that you feel that it might be, so when I say I'd like to talk about my niggers, I say it very fondly at this point.

Clary is my nigger. She's a very realistic human being and she's not a liberal and her being realistic makes me love her even more. Clary's white, but she has a big black birthmark on the back of her left thigh. She used to be ashamed of it until somebody told her that it was beautiful and I think it's because the kid who told her was black. She takes in stray dogs and her house smells like a perfume parlour. When I first went to Clary's house, I thought I was going to have to hold my nose with a clothespin. It's immaculate. It smells better than some of the hospitals I've worked in, never mind the dog hospitals that I've been in which have been cleaner than the state hospital that I worked in, which was Creedmore State Hospital. Clary decided that when God was making her he was painting her and he asked her if she wanted to be born black or white. Clary said to make her white 'cause black folks catch too much hell. They left a black birthmark on the back of her thigh so she would be reminded that she had a choice to be either color, black or white.

One day Clary came to me at the free school and showed me how one has to give when one can't, as well as when one can. Clary says, "Penny, we have a black student in our school. She's a girl. She's fourteen and she needs somebody to relate to, somebody positive, sensitive. Now I talked to her, but I'm white. She needs somebody black to relate to." She couldn't relate to Clary because she was white. I really respected Clary for that. But the first thing I said was that I didn't have the time. I talked about Cor and I talked about Jennings and I went to school to meet this kid because I thought who the hell did I think I was. Nobody ever let me down with my kids. And you know, sometimes we human beings function better absorbin' ourselves in other people's problems. And I was able to try to help this child.

But gettin' back to René, this dead nigger. I know that until the black man makes himself responsible physically, spiritually, and materially for his black sisters, there ain't going to be no freedom and no respect for any of us as a people. When I hear brothers stick their fists up in the air and say "black power," the first thing I ask is "You got babies?" And they say "Yeah," proudly. And I say, "You feedin' them?" And don't let them say no, 'cause black power lies, as far as I'm concerned, in a black baby's full belly.

During those nine months of separation I became friendly with some of the Panther wives of the 21. I call it an honor to have met Cetewayo and Dabruba and Jamal. I have also met some of the others. I was havin' a conversation with one of the Panther wives, and they had gotten to know Lamumba and one of the other children so well. One of the sisters said René was directing and producing a show, and I said, "Well, I don't know where he lives or works," and the sister said, "I'll find out for you." So, I was to go back the next day to this particular Panther pad, which is what Panthers call where they can relax, eat, sleep, whatever, and she gave me a card that said "René Jaques, Information Specialist, ——— Building, 125th & Lenox in Harlem." We call Harlem Leopoldville. The sister who had given me the card had found out where René was and wanted to go along with me. But I knew this was something that I had to do alone.

Circumstances had forced me to find out where this man was. My daughter had had a breakdown and my husband had confiscated her $125 a month from me, her support money. All of us, me, Lamumba, Jennings, and Randy were livin' on $250 a month. I had gone down to Welfare and went through that bullshit down there. I was paying $145 a month for four and a half rooms with three kids and myself and this indifferent social worker came to my house and asked me to move. So, of course, I didn't. The most they wanted to offer me was $50 every two weeks for supplementary help, not taking into consideration that I still had Coretta to cater to on the weekends. I had to take her out, feed her. If I spent Sunday with Cor and we went to the movies, I would have to pay say, like three dollars a ticket to go into a movie house. And I always took Cor's baby sister Randy, right, because she needs her big sister, and because she's the baby, right? I didn't want to leave all of them but I couldn't take all of them, right? So if I went to a movie, it was three dollars for me, three dollars for Clary, three dollars for Cor, and three dollars for

Randy. Twelve dollars to see a movie on a Sunday, and that's why Cor is as sick as she is. This is why she is very hesitant about accepting this so-called "sane" life and even bringin' herself back into it. She don't wanta hear that I don't got no money to take her to the movies or I don't got no money to buy her shoes.

So I had to go to see René. So I walked into his office and I said, "Hey man, like when are you gonna stop preventin' the children's father from taking care of your son?" So we went across the street and talked. I even went out with him to find out if anything was left. And I found out that nothing was left. All the time that I was in love with him, and all the time that I thought we were making love, I was with a dead man. All René is is a fuck. He doesn't make love. If he has any sensitivity, I haven't seen it. I asked him the other day if he had a conscience, and he said he didn't know. This is the first time he'd ever been honest with me.

As a result of going down to see René for some support for Lamumba, I have to go down to Harlem every Thursday to pick up twenty-five dollars. I don't like to go down there. I don't like seein' my people dyin' from drugs. All Harlem is a coffin, one big coffin. All you see is cops and faggots all over the place. You see my people tryin' to survive, tryin' to live, and under the strain I'm under, I can't see it every weekend. And it's an armed camp. If the policemen get a call that a brother is rippin' off a store, you see twenty-five, thirty cop cars goin' toward the area. And if you in the street, look out,

Class No.	AUTHOR SIMMONS, IAN GORDON
List Price	TITLE THE ECOLOGY OF NATURAL RESOURCES
Date Ordered 1-29-75	Edition or Series · Volumes
Date Rec'd.	Place · Publisher · Year Halsted · 1974
Dealer MLS	Recommended by · Fund Charged · Cost HEW
No. of Copies	
Order No.	
L.C. or Wilson Card	

LEBANON VALLEY COLLEGE LIBRARY
ANNVILLE, PENNSYLVANIA 17003

Class No.	AUTHOR	PAINTER, DEANE
List Price 13.95	TITLE	AIR POLLUTION TECHNOLOGY
Date Ordered 1-20-76	Edition or Series	Volumes
Date Rec'd	Place	Publisher Reston	Year 1974
Dealer MLB	Recommended by R.	Fund Charged HEW	Cost
No. of Copies		
Order No.		
L.C. or Wilson Card		

LEBANON VALLEY COLLEGE LIBRARY
ANNVILLE, PENNSYLVANIA 17003

because they don't have any respect for the pedestrian when they decide to have a shootout. So, I'm very fearful of goin' into Harlem. I have to get on those dirty, blood trains and leave my kids, sometimes leave 'em with a babysitter, sometimes leave 'em alone, and go down to Harlem and sit. I've sat six hours, and I dragged Lamumba and Jennings. Six hours. I told the man I was comin' to pick up Lamumba's money. The dude didn't even call into the office to tell me to go home. I finally had to call my girl friend Lola to come and get me.

The baby got filthy in Harlem 'cause Harlem ain't nothin' but a soot pot. You know, the kids were hungry and I was so belittled. It just fucks me around! Why should I have to go through that? I can't even trust the dude to put Lamumba's money in the mail. If I don't catch him on Thursday when he gets paid, the dude will blow the lousy twenty-five dollars a week. I have to go through this nightmare every Thursday and beg this nigger for his twenty-five dollars, you dig it, to feed his child, his child that he insisted, in fact demanded, have his name. I told René not to fuck the kid around and give him his name and then completely and totally reject him. René is a power brother motherfucker dude walkin' around and walkin' through Harlem. Even the junkies say, "Hi Mr. Jaques." They must feel he's a junky, but a clean junky, wherever he might be. I don't know what the fuck he is, but I know Lamumba's bread is comin' from somewhere.

I had to call his main squeeze, meaning his broad who keeps his clothes. I didn't even know she existed when I met René. I just knew another broad existed. I don't know that they're married. They might as well be married since she's given him twenty-five years of her life. I had to call her up and the broad told me on the telephone that she didn't care about me and Lamumba. You know? This is the kind of outrageous thing I had to go through. I had to bug his main squeeze and upset her so much she didn't even go to work. That's how I got René to relate normally to me when I cruised on down to get Lamumba's money. This don't make no sense.

The dude went on vacation for three weeks and I didn't see no money for three weeks. And the motherfucker didn't even reimburse me. You understand? So when the brothers is walkin' around with their fists up, and this is what I told René, they're wearing Brooks Brothers' suits and 'gator shoes and their babies are starving to death. All those power brothers who are eatin' filet mignon and chicken livers, and who don't even eat their vegetables out of the same plate, can take their fists, put 'em on their dicks, and jerk off, 'cause that's where they comin' from.

I don't even want to deal with it. The man knows that I have John in court. He knows that I'm going through all this emotional strain of havin' a child go insane and tryin' to get her to relate to our insane existence. Coretta was sitting at the table eating dinner with us when I was about five months' pregnant with Lamumba and she looked at René very intensely, jumped up from the table and said, "The least you can do is marry her." So this is how much Cor thinks of René. She calls him "the old man." He knows what I'm up against. He knows I'm trying to relocate because the doctor at High Point tells me if I had a larger apartment my Corry could come home. The dude has been playing on my intelligence, playin' on my deep and earnest feeling for the black brother, for the black man, who is so much a part of me. He knows I don't want to go down there and deal with them courts. You stand out there at Family Court, and all you see is sisters takin' brothers to court. The brothers are denyin' the babies and nine times out of ten, if a sister says that you are the father of a baby, you are. She ain't pickin' you out at random. And most black men who see their babies in a nursery for the first time can tell which one belongs to them. There's no guessing about it. It's theirs.

So to deny the child and put the sister through so much humiliation defeats the movement. The sister has to stand before a white judge who is so tired and so fascistic and has preconceived ideas about the inadequacies of the black male. It takes me back to the plantation days when the men were bucks and the women were wenches and the kids were little bucks and wenches. We have to elevate ourselves from what we were considered to be during slavery times. Clary, my white sister, can go to court and get anything she wants because her skin is white. They would have her husband workin' two jobs to give her alimony to give her child support to keep her in the fashion she's used to livin'. But the court caters to the black man's weaknesses. They don't push them sons of bitches. They don't do nothing. Therefore, black kids starve and black mothers go insane because they live in this hell every day, totally alone and unprotected.

I used to think of how René used to make me feel. And I thought when I met him, like he promised me, that nothin' was going to hurt me anymore. You were gonna take care of me. You promised my parents when I was four months' pregnant that you were gonna take care of me. Now, fuck me, man, it's Lamumba. It's Lamumba now. I hope that one day I will be able to guide my emotionally disturbed daughter, to guide my other two children who are feeling very, very rejected now because their father has not seen them for two years. I hope that I can become so self-supporting that Lamumba and I can completely delete you out of our lives.

But as long as I'm gonna pull anybody's coat for some money for Lamumba, it's gonna be René Jaques' coat. Until I can do better for myself. Black men are the only men who put their women on the corner. They're the only men who put the beautiful stuff on the corner. And we were sold into slavery, for money, and we were priceless then and we still are. I'm not defaming all black men. I know dedicated and loving and powerful and good brothers who take care of their crumbsnatchers and their women. But not too many have passed through my life. So to you, René Jaques, I say Lamumba was your second chance, and our conversations on you will end now, and I'm signing off to you, power brother, motherfucker.

14

I WILL be the first person to move from Cunningham Heights without a truck because there's nothing I own that I want. There is nothin' that I could use or is usable anymore. I remember one time the Internal Revenue man came to my house and told me that I owed the government $900, or something like that, in back pay taxes. I couldn't believe my ears. I said, "What taxes?" And he said, "Well, your husband's been paying you $3,600 a year and it's tax-deductible since it is considered income for you." So here I was, bustin' my chops, etc., so I said, "Come right on in. You can have all this garbage in here. 'Cause I don't want it."

I told him that Goodwill would probably charge me to take it out of my apartment. Most of the things I have are second- and third-hand. I refuse to buy anything new. I could get myself in debt and buy three rooms of furniture for about five hundred dollars. By the time I'm finished payin' that and the late charges and the overcharges, the glue will have disconnected from the wood that it's made of. You know, I've got taste, and if I can't have the best, I don't want anything at all.

So what I'm trying to say is that I don't know whether it's out of modesty, I don't think so, but I don't have a monopoly on sad times. Most people have had something very tragic happen to them in their lives. I feel that everybody's problems are as big as mine. They have to deal with their problems just like I have to deal with mine. Actually, I feel very self-conscious talking about my problems. But a lot of things have happened to me. Sometimes I see a commercial come on television with an ex-addict on it, and he talks how he used to be an addict and how this rehabilitation program is helping him, and if it wasn't for the program he don't know what he would have done. I find myself resenting this. I've never been a drudge on society, I've never hurt anyone consciously. I've never been an addict. Must one become negative in our society in our world in order to be noted? Must I become an alcoholic, must I become an addict, must I drop out in order to be noticed?

When I get downtrodden and I get bitter and I get hostile and I get schizoid and I get impatient, and I'm hurt and I feel lost, I just beg and pray to the Supreme Ear. Some of us call him God, some of us call him Allah, some of us call him Jehovah. I don't ask the Supreme Ear to take my cross off my shoulders, to take my burden off my shoulders. I just ask him to shift the weight a little bit because my back is gettin' kinda tired. I have damned the Supreme Ear, cursed him and denied him. But something's kept me going all these years.

It's my crumbsnatchers who have kept me on the road of righteousness in the sense that I'm still hangin' in there. I've been a mother since I was seventeen. I'm not tired of being a mother, I'm just tired of my children needing the bare necessities in life.

When my mother was alive, she used to take a paper bag and use it for writing paper to write down what she wanted for her children. I have paper-bag dreams too. I want to be able to get my children a pair of shoes, not that they need, but possibly a pair that they may want. I'd like to have food in my house in abundance so that it will not remind me of the poverty that I lived in when I was a child. I don't want them to know the hunger, the hunger that was totally unnecessary. I've been so busy being a mother, a father, grandparents, and uncles and aunts to my children, that I hardly ever stop for myself and think of a paper-bag dream for me. The only luxury I have is taking a late-night hot bath, with soap and water, and to oil my body when I come out of the tub.

I want to become totally self-supporting. I want my job to be flexible enough so that when I need to come home to my children, I can without all of us starving to death. Once Lyn Dobrin asked me if she and Arthur could give me fifty dollars a week for Lamumba, and I was very insulted and hurt, but not ungrateful. I told Lyn I didn't need fifty dollars a week, I needed a stake. Stake me, help me finish school and become self-supporting, but don't give me anything. I have pride. Sometimes it's false but most of the time it's righteous pride. I've started college three times since 1968. I've made A's at City College but I've had to stop due to many, many difficulties that the head of a household is responsible for. I want to go to nursing school. I thought about becoming a lawyer but when you have people who depend on you, sometimes you don't have much of a choice to become what you really want to become right then. And I really am a nurse anyway.

I've never wanted to be a star. I've never wanted to be famous. I just wanted to be a good mother, a consistent mother, a responsible mother to the human beings that I brought into this world. I also want to be some man's woman. I want to go to school and complete whatever course I should begin, and not have to come home for any of the main reasons heads of households have to come home. I want to prepare a home for my children and have them all together under the same roof. And that takes money!

I've got to have a break. I've got to be fulfilled. I have enough to give not only to my children but to other people. It's my nature, and there's nothin' I can do about it. It's there. I can't change it. I love people and I find that most people are nice. And when I rant and rave and raise hell about the power structure and about slaverytood, and nigratood, and nigraism, and everything else that befolds me being a black woman every day, I still love people. I still need to give to people.

The hospital that Cor is in upstate New York is surrounded by quite a few country clubs filled with people who live and not just survive. One day I said, "Coretta, don't worry. You gonna come home. We gonna have a house and would you like to join the country club?"

And Cor said, "I want the whole country club, Mommy." So Cor even knows what she wants.

15

ALL HAS not been pain for me. During the year that Cor broke down I met my present husband, T. J. He was my life and my pillar of strength. With one or two exceptions, I have never respected any man in my life before I met T. J. How could I? From the time I was five years old when I was almost raped by a park attendant, to Hercules to John to René, how could I? But T. J. wouldn't let me destroy his manhood and wouldn't let me destroy myself. I had his love, devotion, and I have his beautiful daughter, Noni.

When I met T. J., I was obsessed with going to Port Chester to see Cor at High Point. When we were introduced, my mind and apartment were in such chaos that he told me later that he thought I had been in the middle of moving. If T. J. had not walked into my life I probably would have been dead or a resident at Creedmore. This man has had the iron will and fortitude of a giant. Not many men can weep for a woman's pain. We wept together many times because my pain was too much for me to bear alone. Our relationship was stormy. But T. J. had the strength that man Job in the Bible had to live behind this door in these four and a half rooms with me. Like Bobby Seale says in *Seize the Time,* "When poverty comes in the door, love walks out the window." Ain't that the truth? But T. J. possessed the strength that Job did.

I decided to take advantage of my father's tax dollar and my tax dollar. I applied for welfare. If you want to know what degradation feels like, go to the Long Island City Welfare Center. Any human being who can go through that horrible experience process called "ADC" deserves the red badge of courage. I asked to be placed in the WIN Program (Work Incentive Program). First I was asked by the intake worker why I wanted to go to school. That was a stupid-ass question. I told the social worker that I wanted to be self-supporting and have some pride. I didn't want to be poor. After dealing with the welfare workers I've found that most of them play god with human beings. It took a year but I was finally placed in a nursing school.

I went through three babysitters before I was one-quarter of the way through school. Then one day I was going to quit and T. J. saved me. (This was before we were married.) He said, "I've got to see you finish school because you've never finished anything that you ever started or wanted and I am going to see that you do." He quit his job at a car wash and garage in the Bronx. He cooked for us, washed the clothes, cleaned the apartment, took the kids to the doctor, went to school plays, visited teachers, and held me in one piece.

I was training at St. Joseph's Hospital in Far Rockaway. I had to leave the house at 5:45 every morning and it took me two hours to get there. That's what happens in poverty programs. An awesome obstacle course is made for you and set up for you to give up. Out of fifty-five students, only twenty-nine made it. What I couldn't believe is that when some of the private-paying students found out that the class had some poverty paying students, they said they would not have attended the school. What a mind blower!

I was graduated on November 26, 1972, and received the highest honors for chronic diseases and geriatric nursing. T. J., my father, M'dear, my children, and Gertrude and her children shared in my happiness on that night. I am now a Licensed Practical Nurse for hire.

BUT MY own personal struggle has not been enough for me. I had to do something else for someone else. I've found that dealing with other people's problems is one of the main reasons why I have been able to understand and deal with my own dilemmas.

I called Marketa one evening even though it had been almost a year since I had talked to her. I knew that if anyone in the world was doing something constructive, Marketa was. She had been cross-country performing for migrant workers who pick lettuce, grapes, and whatever else migrant workers pick under such terrible and awesome conditions. She was now working in prisons teaching inmates in a drama workshop. She was going to the Queens House of Detention for Men and the Bronx House of Detention for Men. I asked her if I could join.

I was completely absorbed and overwhelmed by the atmosphere and the whole scene at the prison.

The smell of disinfectant reminded me of Creedmore. The stale air and the closeness and confinement of the steel bars left me drained each time I left. I became aware that police prison officers were victims working twelve to fourteen hours a day. There are approximately 900 prisoners at the Queens House of Detention and there are only 130 officers. The employees at the state hospitals are also overworked. Who suffers most? The patients and the prisoners.

We started our workshop with twenty-two prisoners. Some would come and some would go and we ended up with fifteen serious, dedicated people. But it took a while. These men were desperately trying to find themselves so they could deal with and control their minds. The waste of manhood is incredible. Why this waste? I loved my imprisoned brothers but I also resented them. I resented them because survival is out here on the streets. I know and they know that this system is designed to pound them into dust. But they continue to swing in and out of the prison doors year after year. Most were addicts in prison for armed robbery, petty larceny, and various other drug-related crimes. But I never asked them directly what they were in for. I didn't want to, it cut too deep.

They finally began to trust us. We used total recall and improvisation to loosen things up. At first they wouldn't tell us what they were thinking. Marketa would throw out suggestions like what would they do the day they got out of prison. Everyone was either shooting up dope or buying wine. I knew they were bullshitting. I knew these men have depth, warmth, joy, pain, and sorrow in them. All human beings have the same needs. So at one workshop I showed them what Marketa was asking them to do by going back in time myself and recalling my mother's death struggle. The ice was broken and we all wept.

But if any of them would catch me on one of my bad days and ask me for a cigarette I would say, "Fuck you. You ain't on my budget. I've got four crumbsnatchers at home and damn if you're one of them." Then I'd lash into them because I care. How dare they be dope fiends, how dare they shoot drugs? How dare they keep the sisters manless and the children fatherless? Who gave them the right to fuck up?

When I became pregnant, T. J. got a little nervous. He had been a little paranoiac about my being at the prisons before I was pregnant. But he understood how committed I was and let me do four shows with the promise that I would come home after this.

I had a difficult pregnancy as usual. But this time, twenty-four hours after I gave birth, I had a tube ligation. Yes, I was voluntarily sterilized. I had never thought about having my tubes tied until the day my doctor asked me for my child-bearing history. I started with Coretta, 1958. Then there was Jennings, 1959; Randy, 1962; abortion, 1965; Lamumba, 1969; miscarriage, 1972; and Noni, 1973. That is, Noni Afi Jackson, our love child. "Noni" means "gift of God," "Afi" means "Spiritual Thing" and "Jackson" is there because Jackson had a lot of slaves. "Noni" is Nigerian and "Afi" is

Ghananian. Wow! The lines on the doctor's paper just kept filling up.

It was time to stop. I thought about it. Black women are not supposed to get sterilized. That is something our middle-class and upper-class white sisters do. I thought about genocide and nation-time but to hell with all that garbage. Sixty percent of our black homes are fatherless. As I've said before, black power lies in a black baby's full stomach. T. J. understood. "Let's face it, baby," he said, "you've had your day as far as baby-making is concerned." He wanted me to live and enjoy some of my life and I intend to do this for the next fifty years.

EPILOGUE

IT IS now March, 1974. My supposedly happy next fifty years has started with pain and more testing of my fortitude and durability. Poverty and misunderstanding have separated T. J. and myself. One dilemma after another caused us to lash out at each other.

Now he is gone. Where? I don't know. And I am too exhausted to care.

Thus, now I am manless and my children fatherless again. The only thing that keeps me going is the strength and love I receive from my children and close comrades —Arthur and Lyn Dobrin, Marketa and the company, and the countless other human beings who care for me and my children. Lyn says, "When is it going to stop for you, Penny?" All she and the others can do is to keep adding Band-Aids to the gaping wound.

I don't see my family anymore. I haven't seen my sisters in over two years. They are Jehovah's Witnesses now and have been for a number of years. And as far as they are concerned I am worldly and will not make it to the Kingdom Come. Well, if I can't get a peek at the Kingdom, to make sure that I don't repeat this living hell again, then I guess I won't see the Kingdom Come after all.

My twin brother has remarried for a third time in the past ten years. He has a son now. I haven't seen him in a year and a half. Last I heard he drinks heavily, but he seems to be happy. I wish them all happiness. They have found their escapisms and I can't blame them.

Maybe I will find mine if it is meant to be. Until then, I will deal with my dilemmas head-on.

The tragedy of our lives beginning with Mommy's death has caused us to close each other out; seeing each other reminds us all of our pain.

I haven't seen my parents since my marriage to T. J. I spoke to my father in December, and like he says, he and M'Dear like to hear of progress. Thus, as far as they are concerned, I haven't made any. Sometimes it hurts 'cause I dug having my parents for friends, which we were. All I can say about their attitude is that I'll see them when I am progressive and progressing.

My husband, friend, and comrade, T. J., is gone. I hope for good, but that is up to me. He'll bounce back like a boomerang as long as I let him. Day-to-day struggle and existing tore our "thing" to ribbons. Opening an empty refrigerator day after day got to him. It gets to me also. But I have a purpose in life—to be my children's rock—and since I am all they have, I must "keep on keeping on." There is nothing else I can do, short of yielding to the system's escapisms—dope, liquor, street running, institutionalized religions, and all.

I prefer my way; good, bad, or indifferent, it is the only thing I know. Right now I am fighting to survive honorably.

My main concern is Coretta. She is sixteen years old now. She resides at the New Jersey State Diagnostic Center in Menlo Park, New Jersey.

How and why she is there?

John and his wife agreed to let Coretta live with them. The hospital's recommendation (High Point Hospital) upon her release was that she not come home to me. They felt that I could not handle it. The four and a half rooms haven't gotten any bigger. My husband is gone and I have an additional child. Coretta was discharged from High Point in September, 1973, so happy and full of hope.

John did not agree to take her; his new wife did.

Coretta has gone through hell in the past five months. Her father, the indifferent bastard that he is, would not and could not relate to her. In Coretta's desperate hope to change him, she struck out at his wife. I can't blame her (his wife); she tried. She doesn't come from a life of "struggle," she couldn't cope. But John could have if he wanted to. Coretta struck out negatively because she is a disturbed child.

John makes thirty thousand dollars a year. Lives in a corner house on a nice plot of ground, and wouldn't relate to his first-born child. He made life so unbearable for her that she fought out at him and mostly his wife. The bastard had her arrested for being incorrigible. She was taken to the Burlington County House of Detention for Juveniles. Thanks merciful God that the detention center was not overcrowded; it is only equipped to handle ten girls.

I didn't know where she was until she had been there for three weeks. She is still legally in my custody. Thank God I was too poor to pay five hundred dollars to have the divorce judgment changed giving John custody of Coretta.

The authorities saw through him immediately. He has made no contact in her behalf since he had her taken away. I leave him in the hands of the Supreme Ear because one does reap what one sows.

He did one last evil deed. He took Coretta's support from me. I still maintain a home for her. I've been to

Menlo Park twice to see her already. I am so strung out about my failures in trying to win her trust, which I and everyone else has lost, that I haven't had time to rake his ass over the coals.

I don't have a car so it takes me three hours to get to her and three hours back. Thank God my other children are little soldiers; they keep the home fires burning while I'm gone.

Coretta is being tested now and whatever the staff at the Diagnostic Center recommends I will abide by.

Yes, Coretta needs a superwoman to deal with her. But she is my child. And "there but for the grace of God, go I." I love her, her pain has been mine. Must I sacrifice the other children? Do I have the right? I lose if I take her and I lose if I don't. I don't know where to turn. How many times must a mother give up her child?

My salvation lies in my children's strength and love and especially in their smiles and trust in me.

Jennings is now a freshman at Brooklyn Technical High School. My pride beams every morning as he leaves the house "before day in the mornin'," to make his journey to Brooklyn from Queens. He is truly a manchild. Randy is doing excellent in school, she graduates to Junior High in June. She is a joy, strong and full of confidence and going in a positive direction. Lamumba, my "ballbuster," is quick, intelligent, and full of gusto. Noni Afi is seven months old now. Cutting teeth and shows signs of strength and determination.

My financial status is just in back of the "nearly poor" of America. For six people I live on $4,400 a year. My rent is $180 a month. I still work at both the Bronx and Queens Houses of Detention for men. A labor of love, as I am an assistant drama instructor. But, more than that, I *have learned to love, trust, understand, and accept the inmates as human beings. My pain is far less than theirs. For I know what I have to do when I get up in the morning. Boredom, monotony, and non-existent rehabilitation have wasted thousands of minds behind prison walls.*

I have put in six job applications—three hospitals, three nursing homes. I'm here to tell you there ain't no jobs. Licensed practical nurses are working as aides, that's how bad times are. I am trying to get a job at North Shore Hospital in Manhasset, Long Island. Why? Because they have a nursery where, for a small fee, employees can leave their children and pick them up after work. People ask me how I am going to work with the baby being so young and born with an inguinal hernia. She needs constant care, and I say I have to do something—something beyond $250-a-month child support and $64 bi-weekly from welfare as a supplement. I can't go on like this anymore.

I want to work. I am a good nurse. A damn good nurse. But what do I do with my babies?

The only thing that works for me now is the Twenty-third Psalm in the Bible. How does it go again? "The Lord is my shepherd, I shall not want . . . and yea, though I walk through the valley of the shadow of death. . . ."

But I'm not kidding myself. I've had seventeen jobs in the past eight years. I've had to quit—no babysitter, children's illnesses, Coretta's illness; my illnesses: migraines, rheumatoid arthritis spreading all over my body, lordosis of my spine, another umbilical hernia. I've done just about every kind of menial labor there is. No, "I ain't jivin'."

I lived so many walks of life. And no matter how hard it gets I still say, "Mommy, you didn't die twice so that I might live. So, for myself, my crumbsnatchers, and especially for you, I'll hang in there and live this life of survival so your living and dying would not have been in vain.

"*Oh! Mommy, I miss you. . . .*"